JOHN HENRY, THE STEEL DRIVING MAN

John Henry was a railroad man,
He worked from six 'till five,
"Raise 'em up bullies and let 'em drop down,
I'll beat you to the bottom or die."

John Henry said to his captain:
"You are nothing but a common man,
Before that steam drill shall beat me down,
I'll die with my hammer in my hand."

John Henry said to the Shakers:
"You must listen to my call,
Before that steam drill shall beat me down,
I'll jar these mountains till they fall."

John Henry's captain said to him:
"I believe these mountains are caving in."
John Henry said to his captain: "Oh Lord!"
"That's my hammer you hear in the wind."

John Henry he said to his captain:
"Your money is getting mighty slim,
When I hammer through this old mountain,
Oh Captain will you walk in?"

John Henry's captain came to him
With fifty dollars in his hand,
He laid his hand on his shoulder and said
"This belongs to a steel driving man."

John Henry was hammering on the right side,
The big steam drill on the left,
Before that steam drill could beat him down,
He hammered his fool self to death.

They carried John Henry to the mountains,
From his shoulder his hammer would ring,
She caught on fire by a little blue blaze
I believe these old mountains are caving in.

John Henry was lying on his death bed,
He turned over on his side,
And these were the last words John Henry said
"Bring me a cool drink of water before I die."

John Henry had a little woman,
Her name was Pollie Ann,
He hugged and kissed her just before he died,
Saying, "Pollie, do the very best you can."

John Henry's woman heard he was dead,
She could not rest on her bed,
She got up at midnight, caught that No. 4 train,
"I am going where John Henry fell dead."

They carried John Henry to that new burying ground
His wife all dressed in blue,
She laid her hand on John Henry's cold face,
"John Henry I've been true to you."

Price 5 Cents   W. T. BLANKENSHIP.

Facsimile of an old Printed Version of the
Ballad about John Henry
(See pages 84 and 89.)

JOHN HENRY

TRACKING DOWN A NEGRO LEGEND

BY

GUY B. JOHNSON,

AMS PRESS
NEW YORK

Reprinted from the edition of 1929, Chapel Hill
First AMS EDITION published 1969
Manufactured in the United States of America

Library of Congress Catalogue Card Number: 75-80720

AMS PRESS, INC.
New York, N. Y. 10003

*To Every John Henry Who
Drives the Steel on Down*

PREFACE

THIS VOLUME offers as its reason for being its attempt to describe in some detail one of the most fascinating legends native to America—the legend of John Henry, the Negro steel driver. Whatever the origin of the first beliefs and ballads about John Henry, Negro folk have been almost solely responsible for the preservation and diffusion of the legend, and this work is offered as a sympathetic study of a significant segment of their folklore.

I am well aware that there is more than one way of dealing with a subject of this kind, but I conceive my mission to be to bring together and co-ordinate as much actual folk material as possible and thus lay a foundation for various other approaches to the study of John Henry. I have tried, however, to make the book something more than a mere compilation of data, for I am not one of those who believe that folklore studies must be dull in order to be scientific.

To thank adequately all those who have contributed to this volume would be to write another and a larger volume. I have imposed upon numerous Negro acquaintances in one way or another; I have importuned strangers to tell me what they knew about John Henry; I have held John Henry contests in dozens of Negro schools and colleges; I have benefited by the good will of Negro editors and have sought John Henry data by means of stories, contests, and advertisements in the Negro press. I have also drawn upon numerous white people, especially in my investigations at Big Bend Tunnel. To the Institute for Research in Social Science at the University of North Carolina I am indebted for having made this research possible. To Professor Howard W. Odum I owe gratitude for constant interest in and advice upon the work. Professor Paul Green and Dr. T. J. Woofter, Jr., both of this University, read the manuscript and made helpful suggestions. I hereby express my appreciation.

G. B. J.

Chapel Hill
October 11, 1928.

CONTENTS

Preface vii

I. The John Henry Tradition 1

II. On the Trail of John Henry 8

III. John Henry and Big Bend Tunnel 27

IV. John Henry: Man or Myth? 45

V. John Henry and John Hardy 55

VI. John Henry Hammer Songs 69

VII. John Henry Ballads 84

VIII. John Henry, the Hero 142

Bibliography of John Henry 152

JOHN HENRY

CHAPTER I

THE JOHN HENRY TRADITION

NEGRO SINGERS have celebrated the exploits of so many roustabouts and bad men that one may be pardoned a shock of surprise upon discovering that their greatest idol and hero is not an all-round desperado but a sober steel driver who died "with his hammer in his hand." John Henry is, I suppose, the Negro's greatest folk character. His fame is sung in every nook and corner of the United States where Negroes live, sung oftenest by wanderers and laborers who could tell three times as much about John Henry as they could about Booker T. Washington.

Ask almost any Negro working man who John Henry was, and he will reply with, "He's man beat the steam drill," or "He's best steel driver the world ever afforded," or some such statement. Some will tell a detailed story of how John Henry competed with a steam drill, won the contest, but dropped dead. Others will merely affirm that there was a John Henry and that he did beat a steam drill. Most of them have vague ideas about the time and place of the alleged drilling episode, but whatever they lack in this respect they compensate for in their unshakable belief in the reality of John Henry and his victory over the steam drill. John Henry has become a byword with them, a synonym for superstrength and super-endurance. He is their standard of comparison. They talk him and they sing him as they work and as they loaf.

The songs about John Henry are at the heart of the legend which has sprung up around him. There is the narrative ballad type, sung most frequently as a solo with banjo or guitar accompaniment, of which the following Chapel Hill version is an example:[1]

[1] For the tune see chap. VII, p. 100.

John Henry was a steel-driving man,
Carried his hammer all the time;
Before he'd let the steam drill beat him down,
He'd die with the hammer in his hand,
He'd die with the hammer in his hand.

John Henry said to his captain,
"Well, a man ain't nothing but a man,
And before I'll be beaten by your old steam drill
I'll die with my hammer in my hand,
I'll die with the hammer in my hand."

John Henry had a little woman,
Her name was Polly Ann.
John Henry lay sick down on his bed,
Polly drove steel like a man,
Polly drove steel like a man.

John Henry went to the tunnel,
He beat that steam drill down;
But the rock was tall, poor John was small,
He laid down his hammer and he died,
He laid down his hammer and he died.

The work song type is composed of short lines repeated several times, with pauses intervening for the stroke of pick or hammer and usually sung by a group. Following is a typical John Henry work song, taken from the singing of a group of Negro laborers at Columbia, South Carolina.[2]

If I could hammer
Like John Henry,
If I could hammer
Like John Henry,
Lord, I'd be a man,
Lord, I'd be a man.

[2] For the tune see chap. VI, p. 81.

If I could hammer
Like John Henry,
If I could hammer
Like John Henry,
I'd bro-by, Lord,
I'd bro-by.

Nine-pound hammer
Kill John Henry,
Nine-pound hammer
Kill John Henry,
Won't kill me, babe,
Won't kill me.

I been hammering
All round the mountain,
I been hammering
All round the mountain,
Won't kill me, babe,
Won't kill me.

These stories, narrative ballads, and work songs constitute the John Henry tradition. Beginning some sixty years ago, it is now known in one form or another to about nine-tenths of the Negro population. Many Negroes do not know any songs about John Henry, but it is rare indeed that one finds an adult Negro who cannot give the outlines of the John Henry tradition. And now that the phonograph and the radio are singing his praises, John Henry bids fair to enjoy a still greater prestige.

To all who are interested in folklore and its origin and diffusion, the John Henry tradition presents some problems which are baffling enough to be intensely interesting. First of all, there is the question of the authenticity of the legend. Was John Henry a real person or merely the product of a vivid imagination? This sort of question seems to have a peculiar fascination for the human mind. We are always asking how things got started, whether certain traditions are true or not. Although there is among Negroes a widespread belief in the truth of the John Henry tradition and although several students have attempted to find evidence which would solve the mystery, no one as yet has succeeded in answering the question—Was John Henry man or myth?

Then there are other questions closely related to this one. If John Henry lived in the flesh, how much of the story about him is true? If John Henry was a mythical figure, what gave rise to the stories and songs about him?

There is also the question, especially interesting to students of the ballad, of the relation of John Henry to John Hardy. The trails of these two men cross. Of John Hardy's reality there is no doubt. The records show that he was hanged for murder in McDowell County, West Virginia, in 1894. He was a Negro, a superior steel driver, and was reported to have worked at the Big Bend Tunnel, the place where John Henry's death is often alleged to have occurred. Furthermore, there is a ballad called *John Hardy* which has certain things in common with the ballad of *John Henry*.[3] Was John Henry also John Hardy? Or is there only an accidental relation between these two men and these two ballads?

There are still other questions of equal or greater importance. How and to what extent has the John Henry tradition spread out from the place of origin? What changes has it undergone in the process of diffusion? Why does the legend have such a strong appeal for the rank and file of Negro folk, and why is there a very general disposition to believe it to be true? Finally there is the most important thing of all—the question of what the John Henry legend means to the Negro, how it

[3] When printed in italics as here, the reference is to the ballad, otherwise to John Henry the man.

lives on in his daily life and affects his thoughts, his attitudes, his ambitions.

Here a word should be said about our present knowledge of John Henry. About the only contribution to the subject is the one made by Professor John H. Cox of West Virginia University. Professor Cox was interested in the ballad known as *John Hardy*. John Hardy, we have seen, was a Negro steel driver, and there were certain similarities between the ballad about him and the ballad about John Henry. Because of these facts, Cox concluded that the men John Henry and John Hardy were identical and that the ballads were of common parentage. Naturally he ruled out as mere myth the story of John Henry's death as the result of a steel-driving contest. Later, however, as other authors published more and more versions of John Henry, Cox questioned his first judgment and intimated the strong possibility that the ballads are separate entities.[4] But the problem of the origin of *John Henry* and its exact relation to *John Hardy* was left unsolved. This problem has continued to harass all who have given any thought to it. We shall leave further discussion of this question to a later chapter.

In 1925 Dorothy Scarborough, in her book entitled *On the Trail of Negro Folk-Songs*, commented briefly upon John Henry. She evidently accepted Cox's position, for she referred to "John Henry, or John Hardy, the famous steel driller of West Virginia," and made some other statements which seemed to show that she considered the two men to be the same.[5]

[4] For Cox's data on *John Hardy* and *John Henry*, see *Journal of American Folk-Lore*, XXXII, 505; *Folk-Songs of the South*, pp. 175-88; also his doctor's dissertation, "Folk-Songs from West Virginia," Harvard University Library. His latest contribution is "The Yew Pine Mountain," *American Speech*, February, 1927. In this article he indicates that he has somewhat revised his former opinion.

[5] Pp. 218-22, 248.

While Miss Scarborough published several John Henry work songs and commented upon them, she made no effort to solve any of the problems connected with John Henry.

In 1926 Professor Odum and I devoted a chapter of *Negro Workaday Songs* to John Henry. In the absence of sufficient data in favor of the authenticity of the John Henry legend, we stated that "John Henry . . . was most probably a mythical character."[6] We did, however, disagree with Cox on the question of the relation of John Henry to John Hardy:

> Prof. J. H. Cox traces *John Henry* to a real person, John Hardy, a Negro who had a reputation in West Virginia as a steel driver and who was hanged for murder in 1894. We are inclined to believe that *John Henry* was of separate origin and has become mixed with the John Hardy story in West Virginia. We have never found a Negro who knew the song as *John Hardy,* and we have no versions which mention the circumstance of the murder and execution.[7]

Beyond this we did nothing to clear up the question of the origin of the John Henry tradition and its relation to the John Hardy story except to publish some fifteen variants of *John Henry.*

In a recent magazine article Carl Sandburg published the music and words of a version of *John Henry* with this explanation:

> In Southern work gangs, John Henry is the strong man, or the ridiculous man, or, anyhow, the man worth talking about, having a myth character somewhat like that of Paul Bunyan of the Big Woods of the North. John Henry is related to John Hardy, as balladry goes, but wears brighter bandannas.[8]

[6] P. 221.
[7] *Ibid.,* p. 222 (n).
[8] "Songs of the Old Frontiers," *Country Gentleman,* April, 1927, p. 134.

What the relation between the ballads or the origin of the John Henry legend is, Mr. Sandburg did not attempt to say. In fact, he made no mention of either of the ballads other than that just quoted, but he apparently looks upon John Henry as a mythical character.

Several other writers have from time to time published variants of *John Henry* and *John Hardy,* but for the most part their purpose has been merely to preserve the songs and not to engage in discussions of the problems raised by the songs. As a consequence the puzzles remain unsolved, and the trail of John Henry still beckons to anyone who will follow it. Any thorough study of the legend must certainly take these unanswered questions into account.

In following the trail of John Henry, I have come across numerous persons who know or pretend to know something definite about him. Some of these are old people who claim varying degrees of personal knowledge; others are younger people who have learned the traditions from their elders. Whether or not their stories and opinions are true, they are important. They show the attitudes of the Negro folk toward John Henry, they show the present state of preservation of the John Henry lore in oral tradition, and they may point the way toward the solution of some of the problems mentioned above.

CHAPTER II

ON THE TRAIL OF JOHN HENRY

John Henry was a steel-drivin' man.
He hammered all over this lan'.

THUS BEGINS one of the ballads about John Henry. And judging from the thousand and one different opinions as to where, when, and how John Henry came to his death, the ballad is about right. If John Henry did not hammer "all over this lan'," he must have hammered over a large portion of it, for his trail has many turnings and leads far and wide.

People have a way of speaking positively about this sort of thing. One man will assure you that he knows beyond the shadow of a doubt that John Henry worked and died in Alabama. Another will say, "Why, everybody knows that old John Henry beat the steam drill up at Big Bend Tunnel in West Virginia." Still another will say, "No, John Henry never was in West Virginia." And so it goes. Nearly every southern state has its claim upon John Henry.

But the very inconsistency of some of these John Henry tales makes them alluring. They give us glimpses of the folk mind in the process of creating, enriching, and diffusing an actual legend. Whether John Henry was a flesh-and-blood man or not, there are thousands of Negroes who believe that he was, and many of them can give the intimate details of his career. By word of mouth, songs and stories about this great steel driver are passed on from old to young. Imagination and invention do their part, and the legend blossoms forth in new colors in each succeeding generation.

There are almost as many variations of the different aspects of the John Henry story as there are people who know anything about John Henry. To record them in detail would be an endless task. I shall point out some of the outstanding variations and leave the others to unfold as the account progresses.

Take, for example, the different ideas as to what sort of work John Henry did. Several Negroes have expressed a belief that John Henry was driving steel in a mine or in a quarry when he had his great battle with the steam drill. Still others think that John Henry was not the sort of steel driver who hammered a drill into rock or granite in order to prepare holes for explosives, but one who drove steel spikes into railroad crossties. One man, a student at the Virginia Normal and Industrial Institute, wrote me as follows:

. . . It happens that every summer I go away to work in order to return to school the next fall. Last summer I went to Brooklyn, N. Y., and obtained a job in the Arbuckle Sugar Co. It was there that I met a hard working fellow who sang this song every day, and as a boy I adopted it. The history is thus: John Henry, a spike driver, was working in the North at the time the steam driller was invented. It was taking work from all the drivers, and John Henry bet his boss he could drive the spike faster than the newly invented machine. The people heard about it and came from town to see it. He hummed a tune and drove the spike, he beat the machine but fell dead afterwards in his tracks. His pal continued to sing and ended the song.

Now I am not certain all of this is true but it is as I was told.

Riveting, another form of work which is sometimes classed as steel driving, is thought by some to have been John Henry's line.

Another idea which I have encountered is that John Henry was a pile driver, that is, one who drives piles or posts into the ground in some sort of construction work. My informant was not very clear on the matter, but he thought that the steam machine which was John Henry's undoing was an apparatus so arranged that a weight, lifted by steam power, was let fall upon the top of the pile.

Naturally the beliefs concerning the way John Henry came to his death vary with the type of work he was supposed to be doing. As a general rule, it is held that he competed with a mechanical drill, beat it, and dropped dead "with the hammer in his hand." Here, however, there is some difference of opinion. Some hold that John Henry died immediately after the contest; others think that he collapsed and was taken to his shanty, where he died that night.

An entirely different version has it that John Henry met his death from a blow of his partner's hammer. As one of the songs goes:

> John Henry had a partner,
> He loved to drive steel all the time.
> The first thing he did he let his hammer slip,
> And he killed John Henry dead,
> And he killed John Henry dead.

Some say that his partner held a grudge against him, and so "busted his brains out" to get even with him. Others think that the fatal blow was entirely accidental: John Henry and another man were driving at "doubles," and John Henry somehow got his head in the way of his partner's hammer. Thus the lines of the work song,

> This old hammer
> Killed John Henry,
> Can't kill me, Lord,
> Can't kill me,

may mean one thing to one man and something entirely different to another.

There is another version of John Henry's death: he was killed by a railroad train. Many Negroes think of him as a railroad man; so it is only natural that they believe he died this way. One of the ballads has this stanza:

> They found him early one morning
> A mile and a half from town,
> His head cut off in the driving wheel,
> And his body ain't never been found.

Finally, one occasionally finds the notion that John Henry was a "bad man." The following account came from a young woman of Summerville, Georgia. It traces John Henry from the cradle to the grave, and for once John Henry is pictured dying an ordinary death.

. . . This John Henry song and story has been in our family for twelve years. An old Bachelor came through from Arkansas an spent the night with us he gave us a Ballad of John Henry and a sketch story of his life I remember a little of the story. John Henry was a bright child he had a famous father whom he was named after and when he was a lad nine years old his father was a steel driver. When he died he told his son he wanted him to be a man after him self. John tried to carry out his father's plan the Boss man he worked under Bought him a ten pound hammer to steel drive with before that he would drive nails in the wall for hours at a time. after that he married he had a loving little wife and she was true to him. he taken sick, he had worked his self down. his boss wanted him to work while he was sick. his boss was mean to him when he got able to walk around he went to his Boss man's house he throw his gun on him and told him how cruel he had treated him. his bos Begged for mercy But it was to late. John Henry shot him in the side. This mans people had him J. H. put in penitentary for life. An then he was under another Cruel Boss man this time he taken sick and had to go home his wife taken his place untill he got so low she had to be at his bed side. When he was yet on his death bed the people that stood by him he told them to take care of his wife and child, he had a little boy he named him after him self John Henry. he died soon after that. people came from all parts of the world to see this Famous man John Henry.

Next take the question of John Henry's surname. Of course his full name might have been just John Henry. That is quite possible in view of the fact that John Henry has for more than a hundred years served as full name for any number of Negroes. In Carter Woodson's compilation, *Free Negro Heads of Families in the United States in 1830*, I find eleven men named John Henry. The number, both slave and free, who bore the name must have been many times that large. However, I often ask Negroes what John Henry's surname was. Most of them do not pretend to know, but a few claim to know beyond any doubt. From Utah I learned that John Henry's surname was Dabney. From North Carolina I got his name as John Henry Dula; from West Virginia, John Henry Martin; from Ohio, John Henry Jones; from Virginia, John Henry Brown; from New York, John Henry Whitsett.

What was John Henry's native state? Some say that he was a North Carolinian. Others say he was from South Carolina or Tennessee or Alabama or some other state. I am sure that nearly every southern state has claimed him at one time or another, and there are even those who say that John Henry was from "up north." Some Negroes feel very strongly on this matter of the native state. Mr. Walter Jordan, of New York City, says, "I heard an old-timer say that he once saw a big fight because one man sang that John Henry came from some other place than East Virginia in the stanza:

Some say he came from England,
Some say he came from Spain,

But it's no such thing, he was an East Virginia man,
And he died with the hammer in his hand,
He died with the hammer in his hand."

Thus it goes. Of the making of John Henry stories there is no end. These are only a few examples of the current ideas about John Henry. The interminable variety of other aspects of the John Henry tradition will make themselves apparent later.

And now, in spite of the thousand and one varieties of John Henryism, I must hasten to say again that on the whole the opinion of the Negro folk clusters pretty regularly around the belief that John Henry was the sort of steel driver who "hit the drill on the head," and that he met his death in a railroad tunnel after beating a steam drill.

There are still many men living who claim to have seen John Henry in the flesh. Then there are the sons, daughters, grandsons, granddaughters, nieces, nephews, and what-not of men who knew John Henry. Fortunately for the student of this tradition, John Henry's origin is not so far in the past but that there are persons yet living who might have known him.

The series of documents which follows will speak for that group of people who have something serious or intimate or historical to say about John Henry. These documents portray the John Henry tradition as nothing else can do. They show that John Henry means something to the Negro, and they may point toward the solution of the question of the origin of the John Henry legend.

The following excerpt from a letter written by Miss Willa P. Wood, of Norfolk, Virginia, is a typical expression of faith in the reality of John Henry:

. . . I was born in Roanoke Va near West Va. and as nearly every one in Roanoke will tell you and also in West Va, John Henry really lived years ago he worked in the Big Bend tun-

nel on the C and O road a steel driver that knew no peer I
know no one that knew John Henry personaly but one and
all will agree that he was the greatest steel driver that ever
lived and that he met his Waterloo only when the steam drill
was invented.

W. A. Bates, of Cleveland, Ohio, who styled himself "a
very busy race man from morn till night," wrote as follows:

My father who is 72 years old worked with the original John
Henry (Jones) 41 years ago, and since that time that song has
been sung by thousands of gander dancers.

Further than this Mr. Bates has never enlightened me. His
father is living, it seems, but he is "out West somewhere" and
there is no way of getting in touch with him. For several
months I kept up a correspondence with Bates in the hope of
getting some of the details of his father's story, but this is all
he could tell me. And finally there came the thing I had been
halfway expecting for a long time: My last letter to him was
returned marked, "Gone, left no address." Thus have perished
many of my fondest hopes of finding out the truth about the
"original" John Henry.

Mr. Melvin T. Hairston, of Raleigh, West Virginia, vouches
for the authenticity of the John Henry tradition. Referring to
a news item of mine published in the McDowell, West Virginia, *Times,* he says:

. . . You wanted to know was it a myth or whether it was
true
Yes it was a true song and story
I live in twenty miles of the Big Ben Tunnel where it all happened
I was also Aquainted with one of his nephews
and have talked with one of the men that was turning the
steel for him when the Incendent happened that the song was
composed from.

Now, since the Big Bend Tunnel referred to here was built in 1870-72 the steel-driving contest, if it occurred there, would have to be from fifty-five to fifty-seven years old. But Bates' father worked with the "original" John Henry forty-one years ago. Evidently, then, these two men are not talking about the same John Henry.

Samuel Perkins, an elderly colored man of Morganton, North Carolina, also claims to know something about John Henry's history. He writes:

. . . We Colered peple here have had some who knew John Henry the Steel Driver who put the Tunnell thru on the B. and O. R. R. near Pittesburg Pa. He is not a myth John Crisp Colered of this town has seen John Henry Song starts like this

When John Henry was a Little Boy
Sitting on his farthers Knee
Said the Big Bend Tunnell on the B. O.
Is going to be death of me.

John Henry was dark brown skin. Weight about 180 lbs. He beat the steam drill down about two inches and won, and then fell dead. This happened in 1862. His picture and other data can be seen in the Big Ben Tunnel on the B & O Road today going into Pittsburg.

A later letter from the same man, written for him by a white man, Mr. Walter L. Greene, runs as follows:

With further reference to my letter sometime ago I am herewith giving you more data on John Henry, steel driver.

John Henry was born in Caldwell County. His real name was John Henry Dula. Sam Perkins who has asked me to write you this, made a trip to see an old colored man, Henry Reed who is now living at Glen Alpine and got this information for you. He further states that Henry Reed knew and talked with John Henry when they were working together in Jelico, Tenn. Henry Reed now is about eighty-five years of age.

Here is indeed confusion. There is no Big Bend Tunnel on the "B & O Road." And, if our informant means "C & O Road," then the Big Bend Tunnel *is* located on that line, but it was not built in 1862.

The Reverend J. F. Glaze, a colored minister of Packard, Kentucky, is another who boasts of an intimate knowledge of John Henry. He says,

> While reading The Defender I fine where yo ar Trieing get the True statement a boute John henry. yes the statement is True I am a man that work with John henry I new him and I new his wife I new the little Song he use ter sange. he use ter drive with a man purnd the name of Abe. Burndis. But ther ar borth dead now at that time ther wars men and I wars a boy I pack watter at the Big Bend Turnel where the 2 men druve steale.

I have tried to get further data from the Reverend Glaze, but beyond the following note I have not succeeded in getting him to go:

> . . . as far as the real date of Con Test I cant tell But I will rite to mi Bruther and see if he cant tell But it has Bend a long time and I was just a boy at the time wars packing water fer the men But I will Tri and see if he new the date or a bout the time. But I new his song he Sang all the time so yo rite and tell me price yo pay.

From the Ohio State Penitentiary, Columbus, I received a very interesting contribution to the history of John Henry. I quote it in full:

> Having seen your advertisement in the Chicago Defender, I am answering your request for information, concerning the Old time Hero of the Big Bend Tunnel Days—or Mr. John Henry.

I have succeeded in recalling and piecing together 13 verses, dedicated to such a deserving and spending character, of by gone days. It was necessary to interview a number of Old Timers, of this Penetentiary to get some of the missing words and to verify my recolections; so I only hope it will please you, and be what you wish.

In regards to the reality of John Henry, I would say he was a real live and powerful man, some 50 years ago, and actually died after beating a steam drill. His wife was a very small woman, who loved John Henry with all her heart.

My Grand Father, on my mother's side, was a steel driver, and worked on all the big jobs through out the country, in them days, when steam drills were not so popular. He was always boasting about his prowess with a hammer, claiming none could beat him but John Henry. He used to sing about John Henry, and tell of the old days when hammers and hammer men, could do the work independent of steam drills.

Being pretty young at the time, I can not now recall the stories I heard, but I know John Henry, died some time in the eighties about 1881 or 1882, I'm sure which was a few years before I was born.

I am setting price on this information, I am a prisoner here in the Ohio Penitentiary and without funds, so I will be pleased to except what ever you care to offer.

Mr. Leon R. Harris, of Moline, Illinois, an employee of the Rock Island Railway and secretary of the Rock Island Colored Employees' Club, has the following to say about John Henry in a personal letter:

. . . The ballad, by special right, belongs to the railroad builders. John Henry was a railroad builder. It belongs to the pick-and-shovel men,—to the scraper and wheeler man,—to the skinners,—to the steel drivers, to the men of the railroad construction camps, which they call the "gradin' camp." It is a song by Negro laborers everywhere, but none can sing it as they can sing it, because none honor and revere the memory of John Henry as do they. I have been a "Rambler" all my life,—ever since I ran away from the "white folks" when twelve years old,—and I have worked with my people in railroad grading camps from the Great Lakes to Florida and from the Atlantic to the Missouri River, and, wherever I have worked, I have always found someone who could and would sing of John Henry.

And I have tried faithfully to get the story of John Henry. No folk song fiend has searched more diligently than have I. But I have failed. Anyone who tries will fail. I believe, however, that the following are facts:

1. John Henry really lived.
2. He beat a steam drill down and died doing it.
3. Li'l Bill was his "buddie" or helper.
4. He worked for a railroad construction contractor.
5. His wife, or his woman's name was "Lucy." (I have never heard any other woman's name in a "John Henry" song.)

These are probabilities:

1. He died in the early 70's.
2. He was a Virginian.
3. He worked on the C. & O. road or on a branch of that system.
4. His "captain's" name was Tommy Walters—probably an assistant foreman however.

In a later communication Mr. Harris makes these additional statements:

. . . I have always been deeply interested in John Henry. I knew that his was a story worth preserving and about fifteen years ago I wrote a short story built around the incident, but could never find a publisher. This winter I revised it some and sent it to the Opportunity contest. I got most of my information from an old Negro grader who was called John Camp. This was not his name for I know he was a fugitive from justice. He claimed to have known John Henry personally—said he was present when he died, but he prevaricated so much that I could not believe much that he said was true. He was a good banjoist, and it is his version of the song and tune that I sent. He said that John Henry died during the Civil War, also that he was a "free" Negro—but that is hardly possible for no steam drills were used in this country prior to that time. None that I know of.

From Salt Lake City, Utah, Mr. C. C. Spencer sends a vivid account of John Henry which differs radically from any of the others quoted. This informant's letter reads:

. . . John Henry was a native of Holly Springs, Mississippi, and was shipped to the Cruzee mountain tunnel, Alabama, to work on the A. G. S. Railway in the year of 1880. In 1881 he had acquired such a skill as a hand driller that every one along the road was singing his praise. It happened that at about this time an agent for a steam drill company (drills used now are compressed air) came around trying to sell the contractor a steam drill. The contractor informed the agent that he had a Negro who could beat his damned old drill any day; as a result of this argument the company owning the drill offered to put it in for nothing if this man could drill more rock with the hammer than he could with his drill. And, so the contractor (Shea & Dabner) accepted the proposition.

This man John Henry, whose real name was John H. Dabner, was called to the office and they asked him if he could beat this steam drill. He said that he could, but the fact of the matter was he had never seen a steam drill and did not know what one could do. The contractor told him that if he could beat this steam drill he would give him a new suit of clothes and fifty dollars, which was a large amount for that day and time. John Henry accepted the proposition providing they would buy him a fourteen-pound hammer. This the contractor did.

Now the drills that we had in those days were nothing like the drills we have today. The drills they used then in hard rock could only drill a hole twenty-five feet deep in a day and the average man could only drill a hole about fifteen feet deep in a day working by hand.

Well—preparations were being made for the race for about three weeks, and on the 20th of September, 1882, the race took place, the agent from New York using steam, and the man from Mississippi, using a fourteen-pound hammer, in the hardest rock ever known in Alabama.

The agent had lots of trouble with his drill, but John Henry and his helper (Rubin Johnson) one turning the drill and the other striking, kept pecking away with that old fourteen-pound hammer. Of course the writer was only about fourteen years old at that time, but I remember there were about three or four hundred people present.

When the poor man with the hammer fell in the arms of his helper in a dead faint, they threw water on him and revived him, and his first words were: "send for my wife, I am blind and dying."

They made way for his wife, who took his head in her lap and the last words he said were: "Have I beat that old steam drill?" The record was twenty-seven and one half feet (27½'). The steam drill twenty-one (21'), and the agent lost his steam drill.

Feeling that Mr. Spencer was contributing something important to the history of John Henry, I asked him for more data on certain specific points. He responded as follows:

I have just received your letter and am indeed pleased to know that it was of some assistance to you in writing the history of John Henry.

Now, my Dear Sir, I feel sure that you do not expect one's mind to be clear concerning the minor things which were connected with this story forty-four years after the Actor has passed from the stage. As I kept no diary in those days, I must quote from memory the facts as near as I can recall them.

No. 1. The name of the Railroad was the Alabama Great Southern.

No. 2. His name was John Henry Dabner, but we called him John Henry.

No. 3. I think he was born a slave in the Dabner family.

No. 4. I should judge that he was at least 25 or 26 years old at the time of his death. His weight was near 180 lbs.; his color very dark he was about 5′ 10 or 11 inches in height.

No. 5. I do not recall the name of the County if I ever knew it, but the tunnel is near the line which devides Georgia and Alabama. I was told by the older men that there was a town on the Georgia side by the name of Riseingforn. At that time I was under the care of a white man, the young Master of my people and I was never left to wander around very much, so I never went to this town in Georgia. There was, also, a town fifteen miles to the north in Alabama (in which was an Iron-Ore mine) by the name of "Red Mountain."

Now, Sir, as this Railroad was in the process of construction, there was no train's running upon it, so the names of these towns may have changed ere this time.

No, John Henry never was in West Virginia, but his wife stayed with the older men and cooked for many of them after we came to West Virginia, in 1886, for the purpose of working on the Narfork & Western Railroad in the Elkhorn tunnel.

The above is about all that I know of any importance about John Henry.

. . . John Brown was the man of the "Big Ben tunnel fame." This man lived and probably died before this writer ever came upon the stage. In my younger days I saw old men who claimed to have worked with this man—but no two told me the same story.

This tunnel was put through with slaves, and if John Brown was one of the men who worked there as a slave, or in the Big Ben tunnel at any time, he never raced against a steam drill. There never was a steam drill in there. If you will write to any Railroad Journal you will find that the "C. & O." road was put through in 59-69, long before the steam drills came into use.

This is a trend of the song about John Brown, sang when I was a boy some forty six years ago: "John Brown was a little boy, sitting upon his Mother's knee. He said the Big Ben tunnel on the C. & O. Road will sure be the death of me."

Thus Mr. Spencer tells of his personal knowledge of John Henry. Yet he merely enlarges the mystery when he speaks of "John Brown, the man of Big Ben tunnel fame." Is this John Brown the John Henry about whom the other informants have been talking?

Mr. Spencer's Alabama claims, however, are not entirely without support from other sources. Mr. F. P. Barker, an aged colored man of Birmingham, Alabama, makes the following contribution:

I take great Peasur to write and informing you that there was a real Man John Henry. Brown skin Colord 147 lb a steel driver He driv against a steam drill and beate it down a shaft advancin. He song before He wowed let it beat him down that He wowed die with his Hammer in his Hand and He did it. I F. P. Barker I was driving steel on Red Mountin at that time this Happen about 45 years ago sowm where about that time. Just as true as you see the sun. there was a real man John Henry. He was the champon of wowld with a Hammer. . . . I was Driving steel on Red Mountain at the time of the contest. John Henry was on Cursey Mountain tunnel in His song he told his shaker to shak that drill and turn it around John Henry is Bownd to Beat the steem Drill down the steem Drill Beat men of every other Race down to the sand. Now Ill gaive my life before I let it beat the Negro man. I tell you more a bout it when I see some more of my old mates I am 73 years old and it been nerley a half a cenetery.

From Lansing, Michigan, comes this account of John Henry as the writer, Glendora Cannon Cummings, learned it from her father and her uncle:

I am writing you concerning the history of John Henry. This is my story:

My Uncle Gus (the man who raised my father) was working by John Henry and saw him when he beat the steam drill and fell dead. This was in the year of 1887. It was at Oak Mountain Alabama. They were working for Shay and Dabney, the meanest white contractors at that time.

The steel drivers were the highest salaried men. But John Henry's salary was higher than theirs. Nobody ever drove steel as well as him. I mean when I say the steel drivers were the highest paid; that for a negro in those days in South.

John Henry wielded a nine pound Hammer. So the words of one of the songs: Is: "A nine pound hammer killed John Henry but this old hammer wont kill me." Both my Uncle Gus and my father were steel drivers. So I have heard several different kinds of the John Henry songs. In one John Henry song a man named Lazarus is mentioned, and also George Collins. These people are not myths. They all lived in the camp with my Uncle Gus and my father. My father arrived after John Henry dropped dead, but my Uncle Gus and John Henry were friends.

I have other statements, some of them brief and non-specific —such as, "my father worked with John Henry in Tennessee forty or fifty years ago," or "I know a man whose uncle worked with John Henry up North," etc.—but those already quoted will suffice to show the status of the John Henry tradition among those who claim to have intimate knowledge of him. Such personal documents might be duplicated by anyone who takes up John Henry's trail. There is no way of telling how many people are yet living in this country who worked, or whose father or uncle or grandfather worked, with "the original John Henry." Like tracing the descendants of those who came over on the Mayflower, this sort of thing seems to have no end.

What light do these documents throw upon the question of the origin of the John Henry tradition? When one considers the abnormalities and errors to which the human memory is subject, especially when it is dealing with something far in the past and tinged with the dramatic, one must admit that it is little short of remarkable that the statements quoted above agree as much as they do. All of the statements which purport to give the actual facts about John Henry fall into one of two groups. The first group indicates the Big Bend Tunnel as the place where John Henry won fame and lost his life. The second group points toward some place in northeastern Alabama as the scene of John Henry's great drilling contest.

First, a word about the "Alabama claims." One of my informants gave the place as "Cruzee Mountain Tunnel on the A. G. S. Railway," the time as September, 1882. Another gave the place as "Cursey Mountain Tunnel" and the time as "about 45 years ago"—that is, about 1882. Another gave the place as Oak Mountain and the time as 1887. This last clue differs from the other two. There is an Oak Mountain which lies just to the southeast of Birmingham, but my informant could not say whether this is the right place or not. There may be any number of hills in Alabama known locally as Oak Mountain.

I have looked at numerous maps of Alabama, old and new, but I can find no place marked Cruzee or Cursey Mountain. I have made inquiries through acquaintances and newspapers in Alabama, but so far I have failed to discover any mountain or tunnel of that name. There was a railroad known as the Alabama Great Southern which was organized in 1877. It is now a part of the Southern System. Replying to a query about the tunnels on this division, H. A. Metcalfe, Roadmaster, wrote:

There is no tunnel on the A G S known as Cruzee Tunnel. There is only one on this line and it is known as Lookout Mountain Tunnel.

Is it possible that forty-five years ago there was really a small tunnel on this line known as Cruzee or Cursey Tunnel, and that later it was transformed into an open cut? Such things have been done in railway engineering. However, I consulted Mr. Metcalfe again, with the following result:

I made a special inquiry as to whether any short tunnel existed on this line, the top of which was afterwards cut out, making an open cut, but can find no record of any such tunnel on this line.

It will be recalled that Mr. C. C. Spencer, in his account of John Henry, said that the steel driver's name was Dabner (Dabney) and that he was a native of Holly Springs, Mississippi. I inquired at Holly Springs, and, while I found out nothing about John Henry, I did find that a white family named Dabney lived at Holly Springs; so it is possible that John Henry was born a slave in the possession of this family.

Here is a neat problem in the weighing of evidence and the discovery of truth. In view of the absence of any sort of objective evidence to support these Alabama claims, they must be dismissed as unproved.

What of the Big Bend Tunnel claims? Now there is a real Big Bend Tunnel, and, while there are in the John Henry lore many mistaken ideas as to the location of this tunnel and its date of construction, there is an overwhelming vote favoring it as the place where John Henry beat the steam drill. I believe I am not far wrong when I say that three-fourths of those who make any pretense at all to knowing where John Henry beat the steam drill will say Big Bend Tunnel. Then, too, the John Henry ballads frequently begin with this kind of stanza:

John Henry was a little boy,
Sitting on his mammy's knee,
Said, "The Big Bend Tunnel on the C. and O. Road
Is going to be the death of me,
Going to be the death of me."

I have never seen any such reference to any of the Alabama places mentioned above. Furthermore, the Big Bend Tunnel was built at least ten years before the alleged date of construction of the Cruzee or Cursey Mountain Tunnel in Alabama. It therefore has priority rights.

All in all, John Henry and Big Bend Tunnel are so intimately connected that an investigation of this tunnel is essential to a well-rounded knowledge of John Henry. It is there, if anywhere, that we must look for the origin of the John Henry tradition.

CHAPTER III

JOHN HENRY AND BIG BEND TUNNEL

THE BIG BEND TUNNEL[1] with which we are concerned is located on the Chesapeake and Ohio Railroad in the Allegheny Mountains in Summers County, West Virginia. It lies about nine miles east of Hinton and one mile west of Talcott. Hinton is the county seat, with a population of about five thousand; Talcott is a village of some two hundred people. It was named from Captain Talcott, who was resident engineer during the construction of the tunnel.

Half a mile west of Talcott the Greenbrier River bends sharply southward, meanders through the country for about ten miles, and returns to a point only a little more than a mile from the beginning of the bend. This gave rise to the name "Big Bend." In building the railroad the engineers were confronted with the alternatives of following the river or tunneling a mile and a quarter through the mountain. They decided to tunnel. Work began early in 1870. Late in 1872 track was laid through the tunnel and the first train passed through. About a thousand laborers, most of them Negroes, were employed about the tunnel at one time or another during its construction.

While Big Bend Tunnel is not one of the great tunnels of the world, it was, and is, considered a work of no little magnitude. It was one of the last of the larger tunnels to be put through by hand-drilling, and necessarily a large number of steel drivers had to be employed.

A steel driver, it should be explained, is a man who strikes a steel drill with a heavy hammer so as to sink the drill into

---

[1] The official name of the tunnel, as shown in the lettering over the portals, is Great Bend Tunnel, but one never hears anything but Big Bend, even among the railroad officials themselves.

rock or some other hard substance, thus making a hole into which an explosive can be inserted. A companion worker holds the drill in place and gives it occasional turns to make the cutting edge effective. This man is known as the turner or shaker. Sometimes two drivers work together, alternating in striking the drill on the head. John Henry is reputed to have driven in the "heading" at the east end of the tunnel. The heading is the upper section of a tunnel project. It comprises about a third or a half of the whole vertical cross section of the tunnel. It is obvious that in cutting the heading, drilling must be done on the horizontal. This is very difficult and dangerous work requiring the services of expert steel drivers. Once this small tube or heading has been cut through, it is a relatively simple matter to drill holes downward and blast out the lower section of the tunnel.

Now, John Henry's is not the only tradition which hovers over Big Bend Tunnel. The life there, with its accidents, its camp brawls, its murders, its isolation, made unforgettable impressions upon the workmen. For the Negro laborers, most of them only five years out of slavery, unused to freedom and unweaned from their old superstitions, this life must have had peculiar horrors and fascinations. Many stories arose and continued to live in the memory of those who worked at Big Bend.

There is the story, for instance, told by old settlers at Talcott, about the fate of two Irishmen, brothers, who had worked on the tunnel until its completion. They drew their pay and prepared to return to their home in the East. One of them suggested that for the sake of sentiment they walk through the tunnel once before leaving. The other acquiesced, and they entered at the west end. Just before they reached the east portal a cave-in snuffed out their lives.

Then there is the tale about the man who was trapped in a shaft after he had lit the fuses on thirty or forty charges of powder. When the drillers had prepared a set of holes, work stopped, and the men were hoisted up the shaft in the bucket. The powder man would then set his charges in place, light the fuses, get into the bucket, and give the signal to be raised. On this occasion, so the story goes, he went to the bucket, but something had suddenly gone wrong with the machinery, and he found that he could not be lifted to safety. The heading had not been driven very far from the shaft, so there was no backing away far enough to get out of danger. Death was certain if the explosions came. Keeping a cool head, the man took out his knife, rushed to the fuses, and cut them one by one. The last fuse had burned within an inch of its end.

Such are the stories that one can hear around Big Bend Tunnel today. Every man who worked there has his own stock of tales of days when the tunnel was under construction. Each believes his own stories to be absolutely true and will often make himself the chief actor in them. Each is a bit inclined to discredit the stories told by someone else, unless they happen to be identical with his own. And who can deny that these tales are true, or at any rate based on fact? Certainly enough events took place at Big Bend to furnish material for all kinds of stories. Something of the atmosphere of those days is found in these newspaper items concerning the tunnel taken from the *Border Watchman,* Union, West Virginia.

Stabbing Affair. We learn that the hands on the East approach of the Big Bend Tunnel and those driving the "heading" East from Shaft 1 having knocked out the rock between them tried to knock out each other. Several parties were severely stabbed. We are unable to learn names. (February 22, 1872.)

. . . On the 16th the "heading between the eastern approach and Shaft 1 were driven together. The hands employed on this part of the work are now having a general jollification. . . ." (February 22, 1872.)

Big Bend Tunnel caved in the other day, and injured several persons, though not dangerously. The obstructions were soon removed and the work goes on. Foul air gives much trouble and there is a good deal of sickness among the employees. But 100 feet of heading remains. (May 16, 1872.)

A private letter from Lewisberg, says two negro men were found dead in the woods near that place a few days since. Greenbrier seems to be full of dead negroes they are doubtless men who having been paid off by the C. and O. R. R. are murdered by their companions, on their way home, to secure their money. (May 23, 1872.)

Daylight and Fresh Air at Big Bend.—The Rubicon Passed.
—On Friday last between 10 and 11 o'clock the headings between shaft one and two were driven together and a current of fresh air now passes through the mountain a distance of over one and a quarter miles. Capt. Johnson the contractor was first to pass through. Messrs. John Holden and C. H. Fox were the foremen who had charge of the hands when the opening was made. After the ceremonies of knocking a hole through a mountain were over all parties repaired to head quarters where a barrel of old Bourbon whiskey, was rolled out and a general jollification ensued. All work suspended. Though a few knives and pistols, boney fists and strong sinewy arms were flourished we have no casualties to report. The order was better than is usual on such occasions. The entire Tunnel will be ready for the track on the first of August. (June 6, 1872.)

A tunnel with so many interesting things to its credit might easily have been the birthplace of the John Henry tradition. And, at first glance, it seems a comparatively simple task to go to Big Bend and get from the old settlers the data which would solve many of the problems of the origin of the John Henry lore. But when one considers the difficulties of securing reliable testimony concerning an incident supposed to have happened fifty-seven years ago, one enters the search with a humble heart. A man who knew the John Henry tradition in his childhood may avow that he knows nothing about it. Another of the same age who never heard of John Henry until he was sixty may declare as fervently that he has known of John Henry all his life—yea, even claim to have been close by when John Henry beat the steam drill! Such are the tricks which memory and rationalization play upon us.

Fortunately, a number of people still survive who either helped to build Big Bend Tunnel or were frequently on the scene of construction and were thus in a position to know what went on in the neighborhood. If their reminiscences are taken and are given cautious consideration, they may be of much value in the search for the origin of the John Henry legend.

In February, 1926, when I began to pursue the idea that the Big Bend Tunnel was the place of origin of the John Henry tradition, I sought the advice of Mr. C. W. Johns, Chief Engineer of the Chesapeake and Ohio Railroad. Among other things, Mr. Johns suggested that Mr. C. E. Waugh, of Orange, Virginia, might know something about John Henry. An inquiry brought the following letter:

Yours to hand in regard to the old Darkey John Henry the old song is a true story while i was not present when the contest was made i was then imployed by the same firm wich was C, R, Mason, and Co of Staunton Va it was in the early seventys when the Big Ben was built Machinery was not known in them days all work done by hand the men that drove the headings in the tunels was looked on as a litle above the common labor and got some twenty five cts more pr day than the common labor there was always a rivality between the Irish

and the Darkeys and ofton contest held to deside wich was the
best hammersmon Mike Olery held the championship for
some years but was defeated by the big darky John Henry
about that time the steam drills was introduced and one sent
to the big bend tunnel to try out of course all the hammersmon
did not take kindly to the steam drill and the made everry
effort to down the steam drill so the selected two of their best
men to drive against the drill with a two days test the worked
twelve hours in thm days John Henry drove against the drill
24 hours and won by severel enches but when the contest was
over he colapsed and wear taken to his shanty and Died that
night this story was told to me many times by the contractor
C, R, Mason i was quite a young man at that time imployed
by the same Co for a number of years and was a member of
the firm of Gooch and Waugh for many years and have every
reason to believe the story was true

It was not until June, 1927, however, that I was able to visit
Big Bend Tunnel and personally collect data pertaining to
John Henry. With headquarters at Hinton, I spent four days
interviewing people in the vicinity of the Big Bend Tunnel.
Most of these people were well along in years, having come to
Summers County before or during the construction of Big
Bend Tunnel. I also talked with several younger folk, white
and colored, in order to learn the status of the John Henry
tradition among the present generation.

Although when John Henry was mentioned some barely
recalled the story, not one among those with whom I talked
in the Talcott community had failed to hear of John Henry.
Several times, engaging some person in casual conversation, I
would make a remark about Big Bend Tunnel. In every instance the response was, "Have you heard about the fellow
that beat the steam drill when they were building the tunnel?"
Opinions differed as to the truth of the story, but the story
itself was apparently common property.

What a pity that someone did not make an investigation at Big Bend ten or fifteen years ago! Even five years ago would have made a great difference in the richness of the data available. On every hand people said, "You should have come a few years sooner. Why, just last year old man B—— died, and he was a man who could have told you the truth about this if anybody could." All but a few of those who were in a position to know the details about John Henry in their youth have passed on or are now too feeble in memory to reconstruct the things which might once have been well known to them.

There is the case of Uncle Beverly Standard, for example. This old colored gentleman was every bit of ninety. Thus he could have been thirty or thirty-five when he worked at Big Bend Tunnel. I visited him at his humble little cottage high up on a mountain side overlooking the enchanting Greenbrier River about four miles east of Talcott. His grandson, Herbert Standard, a youth who piloted me on several of my trips into the country around Talcott, accompanied me and acquainted the old man with my mission.

"John Henry, John Henry," Uncle Beverly said, as if he were speaking to himself. After a moment: "Which John Henry do you want to know about? I've known so many John Henry's."

"I want to know about the one who was a steel driver at Big Bend Tunnel," I explained.

"Big Bend Tunnel—John Henry—Yes, seems like I remember." He paused, and a faint smile came over his face, as if he were at the point of recalling something. But the something wouldn't cross the threshold of his memory. He frowned and added, "No, I guess I didn't know anything about that John Henry."

I stayed half an hour, talking about his age, his corn patch, his horse, his view of the river, hoping that he would suddenly recall something about Big Bend Tunnel days. But he did not. As we were driving back to Talcott, Herbert said, "I'm sorry granddaddy couldn't remember any better. I know that he knew a lot about John Henry, because he used to tell us about John Henry and he sang a song about him. I learned the song from him, but now he can't remember the song or John Henry either."

Similarly, the widow of a man who, according to the local tradition, drove steel as John Henry's partner, could or would not recall one thing her husband had ever said about John Henry. Yet her granddaughter said that only a few months previous to this she heard her grandmother speak to someone about the steel-driving episode.

Some of those whom I interviewed gave me nothing of direct value, but in order to make a well-balanced picture I am giving an account of all testimony as I noted it down in the field, whether it was positive, negative, or indifferent.

Mr. Sam Wallace. Mr. Wallace lives on his farm near Lowell, a small community about two miles east of Talcott. He came to Lowell when the railroad was being built. He helped his father build the railroad bridge across the Greenbrier at Lowell. He was about fifteen at the time. He was frequently at the tunnel during construction and knew personally most of the foremen and the leading steel drivers.

"I never heard of John Henry until two years ago," said Mr. Wallace. "I was down at Talcott one day, and some of the men were talking about John Henry. They said that some fellow had been there asking for information about him.[2]

[2] I wonder to what extent collectors have made John Henry famous at Big Bend! I know of at least two others who were trailing John Henry there before I made my visit.

That was the first time I ever heard anything about John Henry."

"Do you think the steel-driving contest happened?" I asked.

"I certainly don't," he replied. "In the first place, if it had happened I would have heard about it at the time because I was at the tunnel a great deal and I knew most of the steel drivers. In the second place, I'm sure there never was any steam drill at the tunnel. No, I think this John Henry stuff is just a tale somebody started."

The Wyant Family. Mrs. Agnes Wyant, aged ninety-two, lives at the west end of Big Bend Tunnel. She was living in the same place when the tunnel was built, and some of her sons worked in the tunnel. Mrs. Wyant had heard of John Henry but could not recall any specific story about him. I summarized the story for her. She puffed at her cob pipe and said, "That sounds like somebody's imagination to me." She said that according to her recollection all of the drilling was done by hand, and she doubted that there was ever a steam drill at the tunnel.

While I was talking with Mrs. Wyant, her son Charlie, aged fifty-seven, who operates the big fans which clear the tunnel of smoke and heat, came in from his work. His mother told him that I was asking about Big Bend Tunnel.

"Well," he said, "I guess you have already heard the tale about the darky that beat the steam drill."

"Yes," I replied eagerly, "That's just what I'm trying to find out about."

"It might have happened," he said, "but I don't believe it did because I doubt very much if they had a steam drill here." However, Mr. Wyant was born in 1870, the year the tunnel was begun, and his knowledge of John Henry was necessarily second-hand. A little later I talked with his brother, aged seventy-three, who lives on a farm about a mile away. He was employed a part of the time at the west end of the tunnel near the Wyant homestead. He had heard of John Henry, but was not certain how long ago he first heard of him. However, he did not know anyone of that name during the construction of the tunnel.

"I can't vouch either way about that drilling contest," he said. "It might have happened, then again it's hard to see how it could have happened. I don't believe anybody really knows whether it happened or not."

Mr. Banks Terry. Mr. Terry, a colored man, aged seventy-two, came to Talcott in 1880 to help arch the tunnel with brick. He says that he used to hear Tom Jefferson, now dead, say that John Henry beat the steam drill.

"Do you believe that he beat it?" I asked.

"I think it is a settled fact," he said. "I worked in the Croton aqueduct tunnel in New York, and I know something about air drills. Steam drills hadn't been used long when they built Big Bend Tunnel, and they were not as good as the air drills we have these days. I don't believe there is any doubt but that John Henry beat the steam drill."

While Mr. Terry was certain that John Henry beat the steam drill, his knowledge was second-hand. He could not give a description of John Henry, nor could he say whether John Henry died as a result of the contest.

Mr. Alex Hughes. Mr. Hughes, a colored man, who lives in Talcott, stated that he has heard of John Henry as far back as he can remember. But as he was only three or four years old at the time of construction of Big Bend Tunnel, he could not recall ever having seen John Henry. He said that he had never given any particular thought to the story and had always thought of it as "just a song somebody made up." He expressed doubt that there was any truth in the John Henry story.

Mr. Cal Evans. Mr. Evans' testimony was about the same as that of Mr. Hughes. He is a colored citizen of Talcott. When the tunnel was under construction he was a youngster, not quite old enough to take part in the work. He thinks there might have been a steel driver there named John Henry, but he never saw him and could remember nothing about him except what he heard later. He stated that while the story *might* be true he was inclined to believe that it was not.

Mr. W. H. Cottle. Mr. Cottle, who resides in Hinton, is a retired engineer. He worked over fifty years on the C. & O. Railroad, receiving a gold medal in recognition of his service. He is seventy-one and was thus a boy of thirteen when work was begun on the tunnel.

"I carried water and tools at the east end of the tunnel," he said. "My father was on the tunnel work, so I worked too."

"Have you ever heard this John Henry tale before?" I asked.

"Oh, yes," he replied, "I have known of it for a long, long time, but I didn't hear it when I was working at the tunnel. I must have heard it after the tunnel was built."

"How long were you employed at the tunnel?"

"I was there all the time during construction, from the fall of 1869 to the fall of 1872. I can't recall ever having known of any driver named John Henry and I can't recall any drilling contest."

"Do you know whether there was ever a steam drill on the job or not?"

"No," he replied, "I can't remember exactly on that point. My impression is that we didn't have a steam drill. Still I seem to recall some sort of steam boiler apparatus at the east end of the tunnel, but I don't remember just what it was for. It might have been used to run a steam drill, but I don't think so."

Mr. William Wimmer. Mr. Wimmer, aged seventy-three, lives four miles east of Hinton. He was formerly an engineer on the Chesapeake and Ohio Railroad and claims the credit of having driven the first locomotive through Big Bend Tunnel. He was fourteen when work was begun on the tunnel. He and his brother, now dead, went from western North Carolina where they had been working on Cowee Tunnel.

"I carried water and steel to shaft number one," said Mr. Wimmer. "That was down toward the west end of the tunnel. I have heard about that steel-driving contest, but I think I must have heard about it some time after the tunnel was finished. I don't believe there ever was a steam drill at the tunnel. However, I wasn't around the east end much, where all this is supposed to have happened."

"Do you think it could have happened without your hearing about it at the time?"

"Well, yes," he said after some hesitation. "You see, these steel-driving contests were pretty common. I don't mean between men and steam drills, but between two pair of drivers. I have seen many a contest in my day. Back in North Carolina I've seen two or three hundred people gather on a Sunday afternoon to see a contest. There'd usually be a wager up. They'd agree to drive a certain depth or a certain length of time, and the winning pair, that is the driver and the turner, would get the money. I've seen them put up two or three hundred dollars on a contest—besides lots of bets by the spectators on the side. Most people who have worked around tunnels or quarries get used to these contests and sort of take them for granted; so I can see how this fellow, John Henry, could have had his contest without raising much stir around camp. Still, since it was a man against a steam drill, it does look as if the news would have spread around pretty well."

Mr. George Hedrick. Mr. Hedrick, who is seventy-four, lives on his farm near the west end of Big Bend Tunnel. He seemed to know a great deal about John Henry and was quite willing to tell me what he knew.

"My father's farm was near the west end of the tunnel; so when they began to build Big Bend Tunnel, father did some work clearing trees and hauling things. I helped him, and so I was around the tunnel a great deal, though I never worked down at the east end where John Henry worked. But I would sometimes go down there, and I have seen John Henry driving steel. He was a powerful man—tall and heavy, but not fat. He was pretty dark, but not coal black, and I'd say he was rather young—around thirty. Sometimes I could hear him singing clear up at our farm. He would sing certain lines over and over, such as

> Can't she drive 'em!
> Can't she drive 'em!

"Now I can't give you the details of the contest between John Henry and the steam drill, because I was not there at the time, but I heard the men talking about it soon afterward, and I am absolutely certain that it happened. It must have been in 1871 or 1872. Just how it all got started I don't know, but there were some bets made, and John Henry drove against the steam drill. I think that either Jeff Davis or Phil Henderson—they were both white men—turned the drill for John Henry."

"Did John Henry beat the drill and die?" I asked.

"Oh, yes, he beat it, but he didn't die then. I can't say when he died."

Mr. John Hedrick. Mr. Hedrick, aged eighty-two, brother of George Hedrick, lives in Hinton. He did not work on the tunnel himself but lived near by and knew many of the foremen and workmen.

"I did not see the contest myself," said Mr. Hedrick, "but I heard the men talking about it right after it took place. It was about 1870 or '71. I think there is no doubt about John Henry beating the steam drill. I have seen him drive, and he was a mighty strong man."

I asked Mr. Hedrick for a personal description of John Henry.

"John Henry was a low, heavy-set man," he said. "He was yellow, weighed about 160, and must have been about thirty years old at the time he was working here."

Mr. Hedrick could not say whether John Henry died after the contest, although his impression was that he did not. He gave the name of John Henry's partner as Wesley Eddleston.

Mr. C. S. (Neal) Miller. Mr. Miller, who is seventy-four, lives on his farm about a mile north along a creek which joins the river near the east end of Big Bend Tunnel.

"I came here when I was seventeen," said Mr. Miller, "It was the spring of 1869. In the fall of that year I began work at Big Bend. I carried water and steel for the gang of drivers at the east end. I would take the drills to the shop and bring them back after they were sharpened. I often saw John Henry, as he was on the gang that I carried water and drills for.

"John Henry was a powerful man. He weighed about 200, was of medium height, was black, and was about thirty years old.

"The contest took place in 1870, as well as I remember. Jeff Davis, a white man, turned the drill for John Henry.

There was a hundred dollar wager up between John Henry's foreman and the man who brought the steam drill.

"The steam drill wasn't very practical. It was operated by an eight horse-power steam engine. The drill was mounted on steel supports something like table legs, and it could be used only where there was a fairly level surface to set it on. The steam came through a pipe from the boiler to the engine. A belt ran from the engine shaft to a pulley on the drill. There was an apparatus to regulate the position of the drill. They would begin with a short drill and go down to its limit; then they would stop and insert a longer drill. The drill turned round and round instead of churning up and down, and this caused a lot of loose gravel around the top of the hole to slide down and pack the drill. Several times during the contest they had to take the drill out of the hole and clean the gravel out. John Henry outdid the power drill pretty easily, because they had so much trouble with it. After the test the steam drill was dismounted and the boiler was used to run a hoisting engine at shaft number one. The test took place at the east portal, and the steam drill was never taken inside the tunnel.

"Now some people say John Henry died because of this test. But he didn't. At least, he didn't drop dead. As well as I remember, though, he took sick and died from fever soon after that."

I asked Mr. Miller if the contest caused much excitement.

"No," he replied. "It was just considered a sort of test on the steam drill. There wasn't any big crowd around to see it. I was going and coming with water and steel, so I saw how they were getting along from time to time, but I didn't get excited over it especially. The test lasted over a part of two days, and the depth was twenty feet, more or less."

At last I had found a man who not only saw John Henry but also saw the contest. Mr. Miller told me all this in a quiet and casual way as we sat on his porch at dusk. He seemed to see John Henry and the steam drill as clearly as if it were only a few years since he had seen them. It was significant, I thought, that he never spoke of the episode as a contest, but as a test.

Now, we might ask, where are we? Was there a John Henry? Did he beat a steam drill at Big Bend Tunnel? Are we any nearer an answer to these questions than we were when we began?

I submit that the foregoing data may be made to prove almost anything in regard to John Henry. For the sake of argument, take the position that there was no steam drill at Big Bend Tunnel and, consequently, no contest.

One might argue as follows. There are only three out of twelve persons included in the above interviews who claim to have seen John Henry. Only one of these three claims to have seen the contest. Nearly all of the others believe that the contest did not occur. One or two of these believe that it might have occurred, but they are basing their judgment on hearsay plus a possibility that the thing could have happened. Why did not Mr. Wallace, who knew the men said to have been John Henry's driving partners, know of the contest? Why did not Mr. Cottle, who, like Mr. Miller, carried water and steel at the east end of the tunnel during the entire period of construction, see the contest or hear about it?

Then there are inconsistencies in the testimony of those three who do believe that the contest took place. One described John Henry as yellow, low, and heavy-set. Another said he was tall and heavy, but not fat, and "pretty dark." Furthermore the three men are not agreed on the time of the contest.

Mr. Miller placed the date as in the latter part of 1870, while Mr. George Hedrick thought it was 1871 or '72. If, as Mr. Miller said, the steam drill was used at the east portal and was never taken inside the tunnel, the date was probably not later than 1870, for the drilling operations were advanced quite a distance beyond the portal by the end of 1870.

Reasoning thus, it is easy to make out a negative case or at least to put the burden of proof upon those who say that John Henry competed with a steam drill.

However, the proponents of John Henry can make out a pretty good case from the evidence presented above. They would take their cue from Mr. Wimmer and Mr. Miller. Mr. Wimmer stated that drilling contests were quite common among hand drivers and that it was, in his opinion, easily possible that John Henry should have contested with a steam drill without creating more than the ordinary comment. Mr. Miller spoke of the affair as a "test" and said that it did not create any great stir or draw a large crowd. If this be true, then it is easy to see how the thing happened without coming to the attention of many people in the community until months, even years, later. As Mr. Wallace was employed at the bridge two miles east of the tunnel his trips to the tunnel must have been rare. He associated with a group entirely different from the one which worked at the tunnel. He knew some of the drivers, such as Jeff Davis, Phil Henderson, Wesley Eddleston, but it might have been that they did not happen to mention John Henry in his presence.

As for Mr. Cottle, who carried steel and water at the east end but knew nothing about the contest, it may be that he was absent from his work at the time of the contest. It is quite possible that after returning to work he heard no direct mention of the drilling affair for the reason that the workmen were "fed up" on it and no longer discussed a thing which was so familiar to them. Or perhaps Mr. Cottle was mistaken about the date at which he began work. Maybe he came late in 1870 after the contest. Did he not recall having seen some sort of steam boiler at the east portal? This might have been the remains of the steam drill after it was discarded.

As for Mr. Evans, Mr. Hughes, the Wyants, and others who had heard of John Henry but doubted the truth of the story, one can say that it is only natural that, not having witnessed the incident and not having heard about it for some time afterward, they tended to doubt the occurrence of such an unusual thing altogether.

On such details as John Henry's exact weight, height, color, age, and the exact time of the contest, it is foolish to expect two people to agree. These things are really not important, not vital points in the evidence.

Thus one can make out a case either for or against the truth of the John Henry tradition on the basis of evidence available at Big Bend Tunnel. Which case is the more logical I cannot say, for there are other things to be considered before a conclusion can be reached with any safety.

CHAPTER IV

JOHN HENRY: MAN OR MYTH?

THIS QUESTION of the authenticity of the John Henry tradition might well be pursued a little further. One always hates to leave such an inquiry suspended in mid-air. From the testimony before us we may or may not believe that John Henry beat the steam drill at Big Bend Tunnel. Everything depends upon the interpretation of the evidence.

Some of the questions which must be answered before a proper judgment can be made are: Were steam drills in use in 1870? Could a man excel a steam drill at that time? How far could a man drill in one day? Was a steam drill used at Big Bend Tunnel?

According to the *New International Encyclopedia,*

The first reciprocating percussion drill was patented by J. J. Couch of Philadelphia, Pa., in March, 1849. In May of the same year Joseph W. Fowle, who had assisted Couch in developing his drill, patented a reciprocating drill of his own invention. The Fowle drill was improved by Charles Burleigh and was first used in the Hoosac Tunnel.[1]

The Hoosac Tunnel was begun in 1855 and was completed in 1873. Steam drills, then, had been invented and had been in actual use in tunneling for some time prior to the construction of Big Bend Tunnel. There was, therefore, the possibility of a steam drill's being used at Big Bend Tunnel.

As for the relative excellence of hand drills, it is impossible to make any conclusive statement, but it is very probable that a good hand driver could out-drill the early steam drills in certain kinds of rock. An old man who had had a long experience with power drills of all kinds told me in West Vir-

[1] 2nd ed., VII, 260-61.

ginia that while he could not pass on the question of whether a steam drill was used at Big Bend or not, he was convinced that John Henry or any other good driver could easily have beaten the early model steam drill. Mr. Walter Jordan, of New York City, who has had a long acquaintance with drills and drillers, wrote me as follows:

The writer has himself often beat a steam or air drill on a down (wet) hole in very soft rock, as the machine would "mud up" and have to be cleaned out every four or five inches. I have often seen a churn drill cut a hole in soft rock where it would be impossible to use a machine.

There was apparently, then, a pretty good chance that a man such as John Henry is said to have been, could have excelled a steam drill in the early days of power drills.

How far a steam drill could cut in an hour or a day, I have been unable to discover. Certain claims, however, as to the depth of John Henry's drive in the fatal contest need attention. The greatest depth I have ever heard mentioned in this connection is twenty-seven feet. Others range down to eight or ten feet. Mr. Miller, whose testimony was given in the preceding chapter, thought that the depth which John Henry drilled was around twenty feet and that the contest extended over a part of two days. One stanza of a John Henry song gives still another depth:

> Well, the man that invented the steam drill
> Thought he was mighty fine,
> John Henry sunk his fourteen feet
> And the steam drill made only nine,
> The steam drill made only nine.

At first glance one is likely to say that twenty-seven feet or even fifteen feet through solid rock in one day is too much for one man—even for John Henry. In this connection, the following account, "Steel Drilling Contests," in *The Engineering Magazine* is relevant:

STEEL DRILLING CONTESTS

Drilling contests have become deservedly popular among miners and the general public throughout the Rocky Mountain region, and the interest taken in these trials usually brings together many of the best known competitive drillers. At the tournament held at the recent session of the Mining Congress at Helena, the records for both single and double-hand drilling were broken; the former by William Shea, of Montana, with 25 5/16 inches, and the latter by Davy and Tague, also of Montana, with 33 5/16 inches. The rock was granite and the time fifteen minutes in each case. Fifteen teams contested for the double-hand honors, and there were thirteen entries for the single-hand championship. Comparisons between the records made at different contests are somewhat uncertain because of variations in the hardness and toughness of the rocks drilled.[2]

One man drilling in granite more than two feet in fifteen minutes! That man, one could easily believe, would have given John Henry a run for his money. If one kept up this pace, that is, about eight and one-half feet an hour, the total depth for a twelve-hour day would be a hundred feet. The Montana man was, of course, putting all he had into fifteen minutes of drilling. John Henry was doing an all-day job. What would be his average for a day? It is hard to say, because there is no ready basis of comparison, but I think that it would not be far wrong to assume that John Henry's average rate for a day was from one-fifth to one-tenth that of the Montana champion for fifteen minutes. On this basis, John Henry could have drilled from ten to twenty feet in a day

[2] September, 1892, p. 886.

of twelve hours. Now the rock at the east portal of Big Bend Tunnel is not quite as hard as granite. Furthermore, John Henry probably worked longer than twelve hours a day. So the stories about his total drilling depth in the steam drill contest take on an atmosphere of reality. If anything, most of the estimates made by John Henry's admirers are too low.

This, however, is somewhat beside the point. It lends a slight amount of support to the affirmative side of the authenticity question, but only indirectly. The real problem after all is: Can it be shown conclusively that a steam drill was or was not tried out at Big Bend Tunnel? I believe I have tried every possible way of finding an answer to this question. I have talked and written to contractors, engineers, railway officials, drill manufacturers, and others, and I have searched through old magazines and newspapers, but I have not yet found what the historians call documentary evidence on one side or the other of this steam drill question.

Mr. C. C. Huntley of Richmond is a retired engineer. He worked at Big Bend Tunnel and was in a position to know what happened there. He has this to say:

I take pleasure in answering your letter and inclose some information. I went to "Big Ben Tunnel" as machinist steam engineer on Aug. 10th, 1870, and left there Oct. 12, 1872, which was completion of the tunnel. There was no steam drill used there, it was at "Lewis" tunnel where the rock was very hard, they used dynamite to blast with. H. D. Whitcomb was chief Engineer of the C. & O. R. R. Major Payton Randolph was assistant engineer, R. H. Talcott was resident engineer at "Big Ben" tunnel. W. R. Johnson was contractor for the work. Nathan Wildman was General Foreman of machinery.

After I left "Big Ben" tunnel I went on the road as locomotive engineer and ran a passenger train twenty-five years. I was on the road forty-seven years. . . .

Mr. C. W. Johns, Chief Engineer of the Chesapeake and Ohio Railroad, says in a personal letter:

The information that we have, and also information furnished by our Mr. J. P. Nelson, who was Engineer on Big Bend Tunnel, indicates that no steam drills were ever used in this tunnel. It appears from our records that steam drills were first introduced in construction on Lewis Tunnel the latter part of April, 1871.

I later consulted with Mr. Johns on the possibility of finding some old reports of engineers and contractors in the Chesapeake and Ohio Railroad files, but all such papers have been destroyed by fire.

Mr. James P. Nelson, special engineer in the valuation department of the Chesapeake and Ohio Railroad, is one of the few men living who had anything to do with the engineering aspects of Big Bend Tunnel. Replying to an inquiry concerning the steam drill problem, he wrote:

I was stationed at Big Bend Tunnel January, 1870, to September of the same year and was Assistant Engineer on handling surveying instruments for Captain Talcott, who was Resident Engineer on that work, and I have known the tunnel since that time. I saw the first shovelfull of earth cast and worked on top of the tunnel and underneath it, day and night, and I have no recollection of a steam drill having been used. So far as I know, it is all hand work and mostly negro labor. Little or no machinery of any kind was used, even in digging the shafts, except towards the end of the work when my recollection is that steam hoists were used. . . .

Mr. J. E. Harding, of the Ingersoll-Rand Company, New York City, took the trouble to look into the engineering literature before venturing an opinion. In a personal letter he writes as follows:

I spent the entire afternoon of yesterday in the library of the A. I. M. E., searching for data on this tunnel. Please note that at the time it was driven, this tunnel was called the Great Bend Tunnel and not the Big Bend Tunnel. It was one of fourteen which the C. & O. R. R. was building at the same time under the direction of Col. Whitcombe, Chief Engineer. In the literature of that day, 1870 to 1873, I found numerous references to the tunnels of the C. & O. R. R., including the Great Bend Tunnel. Much is stated of the difficulties encountered in driving and the ingenuity displayed by Col. Whitcombe in overcoming the troubles incident to soft ground, mud and other causes.

In the entire literature, not a thing is mentioned regarding using any type of machine in these tunnels, either the Great Bend or any of the others which were being driven at the same time. There is the negative evidence in an article on the Nesquehoning Tunnel, driven in 1871 by Mr. J. Dutton Steele, in which he mentions the fact that mechanical drills had previously been used in the Mt. Cenis and the Hoosac Tunnel previous to his use of such machines in the Nesquehoning.

A very careful search, as I stated above, failed to reveal any mention of any mechanical equipment used in any of the C. & O. tunnels at that time. However, it is not at all impossible that some sort of mechanical equipment may have been tried in the Great Bend Tunnel for the reason that the rock encountered in that tunnel was extremely hard in some places. It is also true that if they tried a steam drill in the tunnel, it was bound to be a failure for the reason that in any closed mine working it is next to or quite impossible to use steam driven equipment, owing to the fact that there is no way of carrying away the generated heat. Men working around even a simple steam drill 10 ft. underground, will be parboiled by the heat from the drill, even tho the exhaust may be conducted outside.

The only possibility that I see, is for you to have someone delve into the old records of the C. & O. R. R.—into their company reports at the time the work was going on, where there may be some mention made of the work. Certainly, the technical literature available at the A. I. M. E. library, carries no reference to any mechanical equipment having been used. . . .

Mr. William F. Wilcox, sales engineer, of Atlanta, sends the following opinion:

I note in the Engineering News Record of August 4th your letter asking if steam drills were used on the big Bend Tunnel on the Chesapeake and Ohio Railroad in West Virginia in 1870 to 1873.

I have no knowledge or record of this Tunnel but since I have had experience in driving Tunnels, I take the liberty in answering.

It is very probable that steam drills were used in this Tunnel to some extent, for at this time the piston drills were not as well made as they are today and the type of Air compressors were not as efficient. Therefore most any Tunnel Superintendent would have tried to increase his efficiency by using Steam driven drills. . . .

Was a steam drill tried out at Big Bend Tunnel? I doubt if we are any nearer an answer to that question than when we began. Again it is largely a matter of opinion. One can take the evidence, such as it is, and make it lean either way. On the negative side, one might ask: How in the name of common sense could a steam drill have been taken to Big Bend Tunnel and tried out without coming to the attention of men like Mr. Nelson, who was one of the resident engineers in charge of operations, or Mr. Huntley, who operated a steam hoisting engine at the tunnel during virtually the entire period of construction?

On the other hand, in spite of considerable evidence to the contrary, it might be argued that it is quite probable that a steam drill was tried out at Big Bend. Mr. Johns, Chief Engineer, has been quoted as saying that the records show that a steam drill was used at Lewis Tunnel in April, 1871. Is it not possible that one was taken to Big Bend just before or after this date? It would have been an easy matter for the same company which placed a steam drill at Lewis Tunnel to transport one to Big Bend. It stands to reason that if they sold a steam drill to the contractor at Lewis, they tried to sell one to the Big Bend contractor. The fact that Mr. Nelson, of the Chesapeake and Ohio Railroad engineering staff, did not see any steam drill at Big Bend is not conclusive negative evidence. He was at Big Bend Tunnel, January, 1870, to September of the same year; so there was plenty of time after his departure for a steam drill to have been tested without his knowledge of it. The very fact that no official record exists to confirm the strong tradition concerning the steam drill incident may be turned into an argument in favor of the tradition. The affair would necessarily have been one between the contractor or a sub-contractor and the agent of the steam drill company, and there was no incentive to report such a brief and trivial thing to the railroad officials.

Those who claim to know that the drilling contest took place say that it lasted only a short while and that after the contest or "test" the steam drill was dismantled and thrown aside. The whole thing was thus brief, informal, unofficial. The steam drill agent made no sale. He merely agreed to a test, the machine showed up badly, was perhaps greatly damaged, he lost his chance to sell it, so he threw it away. Such an episode could easily have occurred without coming to the notice of the officials in charge of operations. The unfavorable opinions quoted above have to do with the question of regular or continuous use of a steam drill at Big Bend and need not be taken as refutations of the claim that a steam drill was tried out in a single brief test.

And so on and on, either way you choose to argue. Perhaps the question will never be settled in a definite way. What, then, shall we do with this larger question: Was John Henry a myth? Since it rests upon other questions, it, too, may never be settled. Here are thousands of Negroes and no small number of white people believing that John Henry was a real man and that he beat a steam drill at Big Bend Tunnel. Their faith cannot, of course, be taken as a proof of the reality of John Henry and his contest; yet it might be argued that belief in a legend of this kind must have had a factual basis originally. Here are three or four men (and there are no doubt a few others of whom I do not know) who claim to have seen John Henry and his contest or to have received reliable and first-hand information to the effect that the story about him is true. One of these men[3] based his belief upon what was told him by C. R. Mason, a well-known contractor in his day, who, however, had nothing to do with Big Bend Tunnel and whose information was therefore at least second-hand. Mr. John Hedrick and his brother, Mr. George Hedrick, saw John Henry. They did not see the contest but heard about it afterwards. Just one man, Mr. C. S. Miller, among all those with whom I have come in contact in my investigation, claims to have seen the contest.

One man against the mountain of negative evidence! Were it not for that one man the question might not be so teasing. Mr. Miller's testimony was deliberate and restrained. Talcott people said, "If Neal Miller says it happened, then it must have happened." His description of the steam drill was too accurate to have been imaginary. I made a rough pen sketch of the drill as he described it, and later I found a striking resemblance between this drill and the illustrations of early steam

[3] See letter of Mr. G. E. Waugh, quoted in chap. III.

drills as shown in the *Scientific American* and other magazines in the latter part of the last century. His discussion of the weak points of the steam drill and the reasons for its poor showing at Big Bend sounded like an expert's opinion. He had apparently had first-hand knowledge of a steam drill; yet I could not bring out by questions any evidence that he had ever had an opportunity to observe one unless it were at Big Bend Tunnel.

Perhaps the wisest thing would be to suspend judgment on this question, but, after weighing all of the evidence, I prefer to believe that (1) there was a Negro steel driver named John Henry at Big Bend Tunnel, that (2) he competed with a steam drill in a test of the practicability of the device, and that (3) he probably died soon after the contest, perhaps from fever. Nevertheless, I am not irrevocably wedded to this position, and I hope that this volume will be instrumental in provoking someone to bring to light what I have failed so far to find, namely, some evidence of a documentary sort which will settle the question conclusively.

The question of whether the John Henry legend rests on a factual basis is after all not of much significance. No matter which way it is answered there remains the fact that the legend itself is a reality, a living, functioning thing in the folk life of the Negro.

CHAPTER V

JOHN HENRY AND JOHN HARDY

Assuming that we have decided that there was such a man as John Henry we have now to decide whether he was merely himself or whether he was John Hardy as well as John Henry.

I have indicated in Chapter I that there was a man known as John Hardy whose career, as celebrated in song, bore striking resemblances to that of John Henry. Several years ago Professor Cox[1] became interested in the *John Hardy* ballads. His study led him into the problem of the relation of this ballad to a ballad which has now come to be known as *John Henry*. His discussion of the question needs consideration at this point.[2]

From various persons in West Virginia Cox obtained data concerning John Hardy. Ex-Governor McCorkle contributed a history of John Hardy. His statement in full, as quoted by Cox, is as follows:

He [John Hardy] was a steel-driver, and was famous in the beginning of the building of the C. & O. Railroad. He was also a steel-driver in the beginning of the extension of the N. & W. Railroad. It was about 1872 that he was in this section. This was before the day of steam-drills; and the drill-work was done by two powerful men, who were special steel-drillers. They struck the steel from each side; and as they struck the steel, they sang a song which they improvised as they worked. John Hardy was the most famous steel-driller ever in Southern West Virginia. He was a magnificent specimen of the genus *Homo*, was reported to be six feet two, and

---

[1] See chap. I.

[2] See "John Hardy," *Journal of American Folk-Lore*, XXXII (October-December, 1919), 505-20. This article included five variants of *John Hardy*. In a later work, *Folk-Songs of the South* (1925), he reprinted most of the discussion and brought the total number of variants up to nine.

weighed two hundred and twenty-five or thirty pounds, was straight as an arrow, and was one of the most handsome men in the country, and, as one informant told me, was as "black as a kittle in hell."

Whenever there was any spectacular performance along the lines of drilling, John Hardy was put on the job; and it is said that he could drill more steel than any two men of his day. He was a great gambler, and was notorious all through the country for his luck in gambling. To the dusky sex all through the country, he was the "greatest ever," and he was admired and beloved by all the Negro women from the southern West Virginia line to the C. & O. In addition to this, he could drink more whiskey, sit up all night and drive steel all day, to a greater extent than any man ever known in the country.

The killing in which he made his final exit was a "mixtery" between women, cards, and liquor; and it was understood that it was more of a fight than a murder. I have been unable to find out where he was hung, but have an idea that it was down in the southwest part, near Virginia; but I am not positive about this. In other words, his story is a story of one of the composite characters that so often arise in the land —a man of kind heart, very strong, pleasant in his address, yet a gambler, a roué, a drunkard, and a fierce fighter.

The song is quite famous in the construction-camps; and when they are driving steel in a large camp, the prowess of John Hardy is always sung. I enclose you some verses which are in addition to the ones you sent me. Of course, you understand that all this about John Hardy is merely among the Negroes. I cannot say that the John Hardy that you mention was hung is the same John Hardy of the song; but it may be so, for he was supposed to be in that vicinity when he last exploited himself. He was never an employee of the C. & O. He was an employee of the Virginia contractors, C. R. Mason & Co., and the Langhorn Company.[3]

[3] *Journal of American Folk-Lore*, XXXII, 505-6. See also *Folk-Songs of the South*, pp. 175-76.

Now it is a matter of record that a Negro named John Hardy, a steel driver in the coal mines of southern West Virginia, was hanged for murder at Welch, McDowell County, in January, 1894. Cox quotes statements from various persons who had something to do with the arrest or trial of John Hardy, as well as an official court document ordering his execution. This was twenty-two years after the date mentioned by ex-Governor McCorkle as the time when John Hardy was famous as a steel driver in railroad work. Hence it was necessary for Cox to decide whether these men were the same or not. Mr. McCorkle had said nothing about John Hardy's age; so Cox assumed it to be at least twenty-four or twenty-five. Four estimates of the age of John Hardy, who was executed at Welch in 1894, were obtained. The assistant clerk of the Criminal Court said John Hardy was "about forty"; a constable said "about thirty"; a deputy clerk said, "about twenty-five years old, as well as I could guess him"; a Negro lawyer who was present at the trial said, "about forty years old, or more."

Placing more credence in the statement of the men who put John Hardy's age at forty, on the assumption that there is a tendency for one to underestimate the age of an elderly though still physically strong Negro, Cox concludes that the John Hardy of 1894 could easily have been at "an age considerable in excess of forty." In other words, he decides that the John Hardy of 1872 and the John Hardy of 1894 were very probably the same. As Cox says, "That two men of the same name and race, so nearly alike in physique, habits, and characteristics, should meet the same fate, for the same crime, in the same locality, is hardly believable."

The problem was further complicated by the fact that Cox found a still different John Hardy story current in Fayette

County, to the north of McDowell and adjoining Summers, in which the Big Bend Tunnel is located.

John Hardy, a Negro, worked for Langhorn, a railroad-contractor from Richmond, Va., at the time of the building of the C. & O. Road. Langhorn had a contract for work on the east side of the Big Bend Tunnel, which is in the adjoining county of Summers, to the east of Fayette County; and some other contractor had the work on the west side of the tunnel. This was the time when the steam-driller was first used. Langhorn did not have one, but the contractor on the other side of the tunnel did; and Langhorn made a wager with him that Hardy could, by hand, drill a hole in less time than the steam-drill could. In the contest that followed, Hardy won, but dropped dead on the spot.

This John Hardy, Cox takes to be the same as the other one. He discounts the story of the steel-drilling contest and looks on the name of John Henry as a corruption of John Hardy:

There remains the belief that John Hardy died from the effects of the drilling contest. In answer to inquiries concerning this, ex-Governor McCorkle writes, "You are mistaken when you say John Hardy died from the drilling-contest." In support of the belief, however, there is a ballad called "The Steel Driver," not as yet found in West Virginia, but reported by Shearin in his "Syllabus of Kentucky Folk-Songs," p. 19, as follows:

"The Steel Driver, ii, 4a3b4c3b, II: John Henry, proud of his skill with sledge and hand-drill, competes with a modern steam-drill in Tunnel No. Nine, on the Chesapeake and Ohio Railroad. Defeated, he dies, asking to be buried with his tools at his breast."

The change of name to John Henry, and the victory into a defeat, is not significant, and is easily accounted for by oral transmission. The same process of reasoning as applied here-tofore identifies John Henry with John Hardy, who could not have died at the end of a drilling contest. Most likely the ballad celebrating the prowess of John Hardy gradually, in its earlier making, enhanced that prowess, and, by the natural tendency to a tragic ending, finally sang of his defeat and death.[4]

Thus Cox concludes that John Henry and John Hardy were one, that one being John Hardy, and that the ballads about them are of common parentage. He regards the John Henry songs as forms of the ballad made about John Hardy before he committed the murder.

Now there is much in favor of the conclusion which Cox has reached. When he made his investigation, only one or two John Henry ballads had come to light, and the structure of these was exactly like the structure of the John Hardy ballads. In the absence of data showing the wide diffusion of John Henry lore, it was natural and logical to assume that John Henry and John Hardy were identical.

Within the last few years, however, a great many John Henry songs have been found, and it is now possible to interpret Cox's data in a new light. In fact, Cox himself has recently indicated his belief that his former position is in need of some revision. Writing in *American Speech,* February, 1927, he says:

Is there a cycle of "John Henry" songs entirely apart from and having no connection with the "John Hardy" cycle?

[4] *Journal of American Folk-Lore,* XXXII, 510-11. Cox goes on to show that the steel-drilling contest "could hardly have happened," because steam drills were not widely used and were probably not tried at all by the C. & O. Railroad. I believe, however, I have proved that the use of steam drills by this railroad as early as 1872 was quite possible, indeed probable. See the letter of the Chief Engineer in the preceding chapter in which it is stated that a steam drill was used at Lewis Tunnel in April, 1871.

When the writer of this article published his study on "John Hardy" . . . , the internal evidence of the material at hand pointed to a common origin. Recent investigations, however, seem to cast some doubt on the correctness of that inference.

There are, of course, the following major possibilities in this Henry-Hardy question:

1. There was no such person as John Henry. The name John Henry was merely an accident, a mispronunciation of John Hardy resulting from oral transmission. This is Cox's solution.

2. There was a man known as John Henry who worked as a driller in railroad construction in southern West Virginia about 1872, but he changed his name to John Hardy and went further south to work in the coal mines, coming to his end on the gallows at Welch in 1894.

3. There was a John Henry, and there was also a John Hardy. The former worked on the Chesapeake and Ohio Railroad and won fame among workmen as a steel driver about 1872. The latter worked as a driver in the coal mines and won notoriety by murdering a man in 1893 and getting hanged in 1894. The two men had no connection.

In the light of what has been said in the preceding chapter, the first of these propositions may be dismissed as untenable. The second is more logical than the first, while the third is still more logical than either of the others.

It is very unlikely, I believe, that John Henry changed his name to John Hardy and died on the gallows. The matter of age is important here. My informants at Big Bend Tunnel (see Chapter III) agreed closely on John Henry's age. Mr. John Hedrick, Mr. George Hedrick, and Mr. Neal Miller all made statements to the effect that John Henry was "about thirty" in 1870 or 1871. Now, if I reason as Cox did, arguing that one tends to underestimate the age of a mature Negro who is in good physical condition, I might assume that John Henry was over forty in 1870. He would then have been well over sixty in 1894, the time of the execution. Cox decided that John Hardy might have been over forty, but I doubt if he could contend that Hardy was as old as sixty, for steel drivers, as a rule, do not last that long. The four estimates of Hardy's age in 1894 which he obtained were twenty-five, thirty, forty, and forty. In guesses having such a wide range, it is safest to assume that the true age was somewhere between the extremes. In other words, as nearly as can be told from estimates of the ages of the men, John Henry in 1872 was about the same age as John Hardy in 1894. They could not, then, have been the same man.

The testimony of ex-Governor McCorkle, quoted above from Cox, lends considerable support to the third proposition. From the general tenor of Mr. McCorkle's account, it is evident that he had no first-hand knowledge of his subject. He was merely putting together an interesting account composed of bits of information which he had picked up at various times. Some of this had to do with John Henry, but it was easy for this part of the narrative to become confused with the John Hardy part, especially easy if Mr. McCorkle had not heard enough about John Henry to impress that name upon his memory as distinct from John Hardy. The first part of his narrative was no doubt derived from that body of John Henry lore which is more or less common throughout the southern part of West Virginia. Another part of his letter most likely concerns John Henry: "The song is quite famous in the construction camps; and when they are driving steel in a large camp, the prowess of John Hardy is always sung." I have heard dozens of driving songs and, as far as I know, I have read all that have ever been published by folk-song collectors, but only once have I heard or seen John Hardy's name in one of them. It is always

> This old hammer
> Killed *John Henry*.

Another piece of Cox's testimony is undoubtedly of John Henry descent—that connected with the belief in Fayette County that John Hardy, a Negro who worked at Big Bend Tunnel, competed with a steam drill. "Hardy won, but dropped dead on the spot." Time has no doubt confused the names in the memory of the informant.

The question of the relation between the two ballads is closely connected with, and no less interesting than, the relation between the two men. While Cox has revised his position, he has not yet decided upon the relationship. He formerly looked upon them as being different stages in the evolution of the same ballad. A John Henry ballad was one made about John Hardy before he committed the murder. A mixed or Henry-Hardy song represented a stage midway between John Henry the steel driver and John Hardy the murderer. In a bona fide John Hardy version, the steel-drilling episode had dropped out entirely. Now, from the discussion already given and the argument about to be presented, it will be evident that the ballads have nothing but an accidental relation.

John Henry originated several years before *John Hardy*. Mr. C. C. Spencer, of Salt Lake City, said that he heard a song about "John Brown of Big Ben Tunnel fame" when he was a boy some forty-seven years ago (i.e. about 1881). Professor Henry C. Davis, of the University of South Carolina, in a conversation with the author at Columbia in February, 1927, said, "I am rather certain I heard the John Henry

hammer song in the early nineties—perhaps before 1890." Mr.
C. W. Johns, Chief Engineer of the Chesapeake and Ohio
Railroad, wrote in February, 1926: "One contractor advises
having first heard the song during the construction of the
Cumberland Valley Branch of the L. & N. Railway in 1887
and another first heard it a few years later on the C. & O.
Railway." In all probability *John Henry* was sung even earlier
than 1881, for the incident which made the name famous must
have happened about 1870 or 1871. *John Hardy* could not have
developed before 1894. According to one of Cox's informants,
John Hardy composed a ballad about himself while he was in
jail and sang it on the scaffold before the execution.[5]

John Henry's praises began to be sung during the period of
railroad construction in West Virginia. Thousands of Negro
laborers from all over the country went to West Virginia
and labored for periods long or short in the building of the
Chesapeake and Ohio Railroad and its branches. Sooner or
later most of these men left West Virginia, and hundreds of
them took with them the story of John Henry. Besides a ballad about John Henry which someone had made, there were
dozens of hammer songs which had grown up among the steel
drivers. Thus *John Henry* was taken to the four corners of the
nation. The whole thing was so much in the lives of the
transient construction camp Negroes and so little in the lives
of the native population that *John Henry* was relatively little
known in West Virginia.

Then came *John Hardy,* in 1894. But it never had anything
like the diffusion or the popularity which *John Henry* had, because the era of big railway construction projects was over
and the migratory Negroes had gone. The mechanism for a
wide diffusion was no longer present. This explains the rarity

[5] Cox, *op. cit.,* p. 506.

of *John Hardy* songs outside of the Appalachian area.[6] I have
so far found only one person outside of that area who knows
John Hardy,[7] and he knew both *John Hardy* and *John Henry*
and insisted that the heroes of the songs were separate and
distinct men. Someone may argue that *John Hardy* was un-
popular with Negroes because its hero was a murderer and
came to a tragic end. The argument is not sound, for the
Negro is certainly not particularly inhibited when it comes to
singing about desperadoes and tough characters in general.[8]

When *John Hardy* came on the scene, only a few snatches
of *John Henry* remained in general circulation in West Virginia. Naturally enough, the first stanza of *John Henry* was
the one which stayed longest in the memory. The author of
John Hardy, whether he was Hardy himself or someone else,
must have been familiar with the structure of *John Henry*, for
he cast his product in exactly the same mold. The original
John Hardy probably recounted the events which led up to
Hardy's execution, saying nothing about Big Bend Tunnel or
a steel-driving contest. But when the new ballad began to cir-
culate, it kept running into *John Henry*. Here and there, a
singer, recalling something from *John Henry* and seeing that
the songs were of the same structure, inserted one or more
John Henry stanzas. This I submit as the explanation of the
mixed versions of *John Hardy* which Cox has found. Of the
nine variants which he has published,[9] five contain bona fide
John Henry stanzas; one is a John Henry song throughout,

[6] *John Hardy* seems to have been largely taken over by whites. All of Cox's
versions were obtained from whites. All of my *John Henry* songs came from
Negroes, with the exception of a few fragments.

[7] R. W. Gordon has, I believe, found two or three scattered versions of
John Hardy. One of these was from California and was published in his
department, "Old Songs that Men Have Sung," in *Adventure Magazine*.

[8] Witness *Jesse James, Railroad Bill, Duncan and Brady*, etc. See *The Negro
and His Songs, Negro Workaday Songs, The American Song Bag*, etc.

[9] For all these, see his *Folk-Songs of the South*, pp. 178-88.

wearing the name of John Henry in most of its stanzas; and only three are bona fide *John Hardy* songs. In the mixed songs, the *John Henry* stanza which occurs most frequently is the usual opening stanza of the *John Henry* ballads, in which John Henry said when he was a little babe that the Big Bend Tunnel was to be the death of him. A variant of this stanza occurs at the opening of four of Cox's versions.

In the version which ex-Governor McCorkle contributed to Cox's collection there occurs a very interesting lapse into John Henryism. The first three stanzas are as follows:

> John Hardy was a bad, bad man,
> He came from a bad, bad land;
> He killed two men in a Shawnee camp,
> Cause he's too damn nervy for to run, God damn!
> Too damn nervy for to run.

> John Hardy went to the rock quarrie,
> He went there for to drive, Lord, Lord!
> The rock was so hard and the steel so soft,
> That he laid down his hammer and he cried,
>   "O my God!"
> He laid down his hammer and he cried.

> John Henry was standing on my right-hand side,
> The steel hammers on my left, Lord, Lord!
> "Before I'd let the steamer beat me down,
> I'd die with my hammer in my hand, by God!
> I'd die with my hammer in my hand."[10]

The rest of the ballad tells about John Hardy's drinking and gambling, his arrest, etc. The first stanza, above, is a *John Hardy* stanza; the second is typically *John Henry* but bears Hardy's name; the third is *John Henry* and bears John

[10] *Ibid.*, p. 178.

Henry's name![11] Evidently the ex-Governor had known some John Henry lines in earlier days, and the name itself bobbed up inadvertently in what he thought was a *John Hardy* stanza.

Additional evidence that the two ballads are entirely separate is found in a comparison of the known tunes to which they are sung. Including the tunes of *John Henry* which are published in this volume, there are now available some fifteen in all. This does not, of course, include hammer songs, their structure being different from the ballads. Of *John Hardy* tunes, only two are available. Unfortunately Cox could not obtain the music for any of his versions. Campbell and Sharp published a *John Hardy* tune.[12] Another, an excellent and authentic folk production, is available on a Columbia phonograph record.[13] The latter is reproduced in Chapter VII. Now the various *John Henry* tunes[14] show quite a range of musical variation; yet none of them overlaps significantly with any of the *John Hardy* tunes. The two *Hardy* tunes are practically identical, and, if they are typical, they indicate that the tunes of the two ballads are not closely related. The tune is an integral part of a ballad, and it is likely to survive the process of ballad transmission as well as or better than the words themselves. If these two ballads had a common origin we should expect to find instances of their tunes being interchanged. No such instances have been found. Thus we have an additional argument in favor of the separateness of the two ballads.

A still greater difference, however, is seen in their rhythms. *John Hardy* is simple, deliberate, and puts one in mind of the

[11] Thinking that the "John Henry" in the third stanza might be a misprint, I made inquiry of Professor Cox, who says that it is printed as it appears on the original manuscript.

[12] *English Folk Songs from the Southern Appalachians*, pp. 257-58.

[13] John Hardy, no. 167-D.

[14] See chap. VII.

conventional English ballad sung by the white mountain people. *John Henry* is faster, is syncopated, and is much more typically Negroid than *John Hardy*.

The foregoing discussion might be summarized as follows:

1. John Henry and John Hardy were separate men.

2. *John Henry* originated earlier than *John Hardy*. This is proved in part by (a) statements of various persons as to the earliest date they heard *John Henry*, but (b) especially by the wider geographical diffusion of *John Henry*.

3. *John Hardy* was patterned after *John Henry*. Both ballads were circulating in the same region, with the result that they often were confused. This explains the fact that five of the nine variants published by Cox were either *John Henry* versions or mixed *Henry-Hardy* versions.

4. The tunes and rhythms of the ballads, as far as can be judged at present, are different.

5. Therefore, the ballads as well as the men are separate entities.

There is one other thing which might be pointed out before John Hardy is dismissed. Although his color, his crime, the time and place of execution are matters of historical verifiability, conflicting stories have grown up about him. Cox reported one of these:

He [Mr. H. S. Walker, of Fayette County] told me, also, that there is a current report in this part of the State concerning a John Hardy who was a tough, a saloon frequenter, an outlaw, and a sort of a thug. He *thinks* this John Hardy was a white man, and he is *sure* that he was hanged later on for killing a man in McDowell County or across the line in Virginia.[15]

I add the following excerpt from a letter which came from Union, West Virginia, as a result of my inquiry about John

[15] *Journal of American Folk-Lore*, XXXII, 510.

Henry and John Hardy, published in the Monroe *Watchman* (Union, West Virginia) in September, 1927:

> I notice in the Monroe Watchman you want to no who John Henry is I do not no a thing about him but I do no a bout John Hardy he was Hanged at Grundy Va. Buckhanan Co not Welch W. Va he killed George Manntz over his wife I was Borned and Raised near Grundy Va and also he was a white man the law allows No Negroes in that county someone can give you something about John Henry hope this will be a help to you. They is a song a bout John Henry I suppose you have heard it John Henry was a steal driving man.

Perhaps there was a white man of similar name who was executed in Virginia.[16] But here are two persons—and there must be many others—who respond with this sort of story when anyone asks them about John Hardy. If these reports can arise in the face of the facts about John Hardy, need we be surprised at the conflicting stories about John Henry? Truly, one can accept some of the John Henry "historical" data with more faith after one has studied John Hardy.

---

* Since this was written I have received the following letter from George W. Mullins, Clerk of Court, Grundy, Va.: "In answer to your inquirey beg to say that John Harding was hanged here on December the 17th, 1897, and that I was present and witnessed the execution. He was the first and only man that I ever seen hanged, and in fact he was the only person ever hanged in this County. He was a white man and was convicted of killing his uncle."

CHAPTER VI

JOHN HENRY HAMMER SONGS

THE WORK SONG type of *John Henry* probably antedated the ballad type. The wide diffusion of certain stanzas found in the work songs shows that they have been a part of the Negro laborer's repertoire for as long a time as the ballad itself. It is an interesting fact that a belief held locally at Big Bend Tunnel has it that as soon as John Henry fell, his partner took up his hammer and went on driving, singing,

> This old hammer
> Killed John Henry,
> Can't kill me, Lord,
> Can't kill me.

—which, of course, is mere legend. But it brings to mind the possibility that the John Henry hammer song could have sprung up almost immediately after the hero's demise, whereas the ballad type required more time in the making.

Wherever Negroes drive steel or dig or do any sort of work that requires regular muscular movements, the chances are that they sing as they work. The chances are, further, that they don't sing very long without mentioning John Henry in one way or another. The very essence of the work song is its fluidity, its adaptability to various kinds and speeds of work. If a worker has any thoughts on John Henry, it is easy for him to put them into his song. Many work songs are spontaneous, sung once and then forgotten. But on the whole they tend to be frequently repeated, and if any particular stanza is interesting it will be taken up by those who hear it and will soon be on its way to general favor among workmen.

There are very few if any work songs confined to John Henry alone. A work song is likely to ramble from nowhere to everywhere before it ends, but John Henry comes in for his full share of verses in the Negro's work songs. Being the hero of the hammer, he naturally is frequently in the thoughts of those who do hammer work. There is something of reverence, overcast with egotism, in

> This old hammer
> Killed John Henry,
> Can't kill me, Lord,
> Can't kill me.

The following John Henry work songs are only a few of the hundreds which might be found, but they represent all the major types of work songs, and they include practically all of the John Henry stanzas which have any considerable diffusion. Wherever possible I have obtained the tunes of the songs. The reader will understand, of course, that a work song tune cannot be recorded with absolute accuracy—or, perhaps, should not be so recorded. If accuracy of time and rhythm is made the goal, the notation becomes confusing, for the length of the measures or units in a work song is apt to vary greatly. The sung parts of the cycle are very regular indeed, but the intervals of rest are often very irregular. The most satisfactory way to note the tunes of these songs, then, is to treat the sung parts as the temporal units and to write the songs in regular tempo.

No description of the harmonic and rhythmic beauties of the Negro work song can do the subject justice. The concerted movements, the grunts emerging at each stroke of pick or hammer, the off-pitch, slurring, sliding attacks made on the tones, the unsteady harmonic patterns—these have to be seen and heard in order to be understood. But if one is interested in learning something about work songs and has no opportunity to observe them in their natural state, let him try his own hand at a pickaxe or a nine-pound hammer, and he will

learn more in ten minutes than he would by reading a volume
of descriptive material.

A

While I was at Big Bend Tunnel I obtained the following
hammer song from Thaddeus Campbell and Herbert Standard, Negro youths who helped me in my investigation. This
is supposed to be the song which John Henry himself sang
when he drove steel. There were other verses, my informants
said, but they had been forgotten.

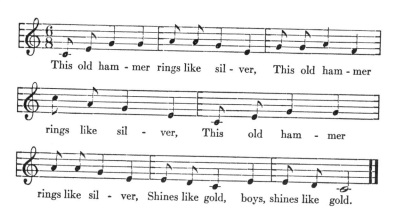

This old ham - mer rings like sil - ver, This old ham - mer
rings like sil - ver, This old ham - mer
rings like sil - ver, Shines like gold, boys, shines like gold.

> This old hammer
> Rings like silver,
> This old hammer
> Rings like silver,
> This old hammer
> Rings like silver,
> Shines like gold, boys,
> Shines like gold.
>
> Ain't no hammer
> In these mountains,
> Ain't no hammer
> In these mountains,

Ain't no hammer
In these mountains,
Rings like mine, boys,
Rings like mine.

Take this hammer,
Take it to the captain;
Take this hammer,
Take it to the captain;
Take this hammer,
Take it to the captain;
Tell him I'm gone, boys,
Tell him I'm gone.

B

A very similar hammer song was communicated by Miss
Willa P. Wood, of Norfolk, Virginia. Miss Wood reports that
she first learned *John Henry* in Roanoke, Virginia. According
to her, the first two stanzas were sung by John Henry, while
the third was sung by his partner just after John Henry
dropped "with the hammer in his hand." The first two lines
of each stanza are sung three times, as in the preceding song.

Ain't no hammer
In this mountain
Outrings mine, boys,
Outrings mine.

Take this hammer,
Give it to the boss man,
Tell him I'm gone, boys,
Tell him I'm gone.

This old hammer
Killed John Henry
But it won't kill me, boys,
It won't kill me.

C

This work song is unusual in its length and in the fact that it sticks to the subject of John Henry throughout. It was communicated in 1927 by Junius E. Byrd, who was at that time studying at Virginia Normal and Industrial Institute. He learned it from a fellow-worker in the summer of 1926 while employed by the Arbuckle Sugar Company, Brooklyn, New York.

Old John Henry
Got to find a job,
Old John Henry
Got to find a job,
Dat steam driller's here,
Here a good man to rob.

Lordy, Lord,
Why did you send dat steam?
Lordy, Lord,
Why did you send dat steam?
It's caused de boss man to run me,
Run me like a oxyen team.

Boss man, listen,
Listen to my plea.
Boss man, listen,
Listen to my plea.
I'll work half de night
If you just let me be.

Got a wife and a child
Waiting for me at de fire.
Got a wife and a child
Waiting for me at de fire.
If I don't work
Ain't no way dey can smile.

Tomorrow at sunrise
I am goin' be a natural man.
Tomorrow at sunrise
I am goin' be a natural man.
Goin' take dat hammer, drive dat
Spike de fastest in de land.

Boss man said,
"You'll never beat dat steam."
Boss man said,
"You'll never beat dat steam."
"But if I don't beat it,
I'll be your slave till I'm lean."

Tell 'em all come,
Come from town to see,
Tell 'em all come,
Come from town to see
Old John Henry drive dat spike
With one, two, three.

Old John Henry
Took dat hammer with thousand around.
Old John Henry
Took dat hammer with thousand around.
Bound to tell you,
Wa'n't a single man in town.

Goin' take dis hammer,
Sing a hobo's tune.
Goin' take dis hammer,
Sing a hobo's tune.
If I fail,
Three human bodies I win.[1]

When you're far from home,
Find yourself alone,
When you're far from home,

[1] Probably a corruption of "three hundred dollars I lose."

Find yourself alone,
Get a old sledge hammer,
Drill your way back home.

Some think it hard,
Tain't hard to me,
Some think it hard,
Tain't hard to me,
Get a buddy to hold it,
Drive it till you can't hardly see.

Dat old steam driller
Long ways behind,
Dat old steam driller
Long ways behind,
But old John Henry
Goin' bring dat spike in on time.

Dat old hammer
Put John Henry in his grave.
Dat old hammer
Put John Henry in his grave.
Lordy, Lord, dis one man
It ain't goin' make dead.

Old John Henry
Gone to his far bound home.
Old John Henry
Gone to his far bound home.
Never to return,
Dat spike he'll never moan.

D

The next is a hammer song as sung by Willie Wilson, a student in Benedict College, Columbia, South Carolina. This tune, by the way, is very common among Negro work gangs in the South. It is the tune which usually accompanies that remarkable work song stanza,[2]

[2] See *Negro Workaday Songs,* pp. 2, 249. It was this stanza which suggested to Professor Odum the title of his book, *Rainbow Round My Shoulder.*

I got a rainbow,
Rainbow round my shoulder,
I got a rainbow,
Rainbow round my shoulder.
Ain't gonna rain,
Lawd, Lawd, ain't gonna rain.

This   is   the   ham - mer,   ham - mer   killed   John

Hen - ry.   This is the ham - mer ham - mer killed John

Hen - ry,   Won't kill me,   Lawd, Lawd, won't kill me.

This is the hammer,
Hammer killed John Henry.
This is the hammer,
Hammer killed John Henry.
Won't kill me.
Lawd, Lawd, won't kill me.

Take this hammer,
Hammer to the captain, *etc.*
Tell him I'm gone,
Lawd, Lawd, tell him I'm gone.

Take this hammer,
Throw it in the river, *etc.*
It'll ring right on,
Lawd, Lawd, ring right on.

Gonna take this hammer,
Ring it on till it strike five, *etc.*
Then go home,
Lawd, Lawd, then go home.

E

Mr. Howard B. Thompson, formerly a student at Virginia
Normal and Industrial Institute, contributes this hammer song.
He writes: "I remember these verses from childhood. Anyone
who has heard the ringing of a hammer when driving steel
at spaced intermissions will be quick to get the tune of this
song. The *heh* should be delivered in a hacking tone expelled
with force."

Thought I heard—heh!
De hammer ringing—heh!
In Big Ben Tunnel—heh!
In Big Ben Tunnel—heh!
Ring so loud—heh!
Ring so loud—heh!

Thought I heard—heh!
Somebody saying—heh!
"Tain't no hammer—heh!
In dis mountain—heh!
Ring like mine—heh!
Ring like mine—heh!"

Ol' John Henry—heh!
Ol' John Henry—heh!
Fell wid de hammer—heh!
Fell wid de hammer—heh!
In his han'—heh!
In his han'—heh!

Dat ol' hammer—heh!
Dat ol' hammer—heh!
Dat killed John Henry—heh!

Dat killed John Henry—heh!
Won' kill me—heh!
Won' kill me—heh!

Ol' John Henry—heh!
Ol' John Henry—heh!
Died wid de hammer—heh!
Died wid de hammer—heh!
In his han'—heh!
In his han'—heh!

Dat ten pound hammer—heh!
Dat ten pound hammer—heh!
Dat killed John Henry—heh!
Dat killed John Henry—heh!
Won' kill me—heh!
Won' kill me—heh!

F

Mr. A. L. Scrivens, Indianola, Mississippi, does not believe in John Henry, but he sent me the following work song which, he says, is "the song of John Henry—complete." The irregularities are typical of the improvised type of work song.

This is the hammer
That kill John Henry,
Kill him dead,
Kill him dead,
Kill him dead.

O John Henry,
O John Henry,
Killed him dead, *etc.*

This old hammer
Of John Henry,
Hear it ring, *etc.*

Take a man
To use this hammer,
Take a man
Like John Henry, *etc.*

This old hammer
Of John Henry
Will kill you dead, *etc.*

Old John Henry
Died like a man,
Died like a man
With that old hammer
In his hand.

Old John Henry
Is my partner,
Died like a man, *etc.*

Can you hear me
Knock John Henry
On this hammer? *etc.*

This old hammer
Of John Henry
Will kill me dead, *etc.*

G

The Nine-Pound Hammer, Brunswick Record No. 177-A, is an excellent work song. Although it is sung by a quartet in regular tempo, one can easily make a hammer song out of it by inserting appropriate pauses, hammer strokes, and grunts. I quote here by permission the chorus of the song and a stanza which refers to John Henry:

Nine-pound hammer
Killed John Henry,
Ain't a-gonna kill me,
Ain't a-gonna kill me.

Chorus

O roll 'em along, buddy,
Don't you roll 'em so slow.
Baby, how can I roll,
When the wheel won't go?

H

Professor Reed Smith, of the University of South Carolina, sang for me one stanza of a work song which he heard when he was a boy.

This old hammer
Killed John Henry,
Killed my brother,
Can't kill me.

I

I repeat here with music one stanza of the work song quoted in Chapter I. It came from a work gang at Columbia, South Carolina. For other stanzas, see Chapter I. This rather weird tune is the kind that workmen like to improvise.

If I could hammer
Like John Henry,
If I could hammer

Like John Henry,
Lawd, I'd be a man,
Lawd, I'd be a man.

J

This fragment was reported by Leon R. Harris, of Moline, Illinois.

O Big Bend Tunnel,
Big Bend Tunnel,
Big Bend Tunnel,
C. & O. Road.

This old hammer
Killed John Henry,
Killed him dead,
Killed him dead.

K

This fragment came from A. C. Dupree, Cleveland, Ohio.

Twelve-pound hammer
Kill John Henry,
Never kill me, baby,
Never kill me.

This is the hammer
Kill John Henry,
Never kill me, baby,
Never kill me.

The above songs will suffice to show the range of words and tunes of the John Henry hammer songs. I have other variants and fragments from Chapel Hill, North Carolina; Columbia, South Carolina; Greenville, South Carolina; Union, West Virginia; New York City. In *Negro Workaday Songs* will be found the words of four John Henry work songs. Dorothy

Scarborough's *On the Trail of Negro Folk-Songs*,[3] contains two or three hammer-song versions of John Henry. "Ever Since Uncle John Henry Been Dead," in Carl Sandburg's *American Songbag,* is also a good example of the hammer song. Other references may be found in the bibliography.

[3] Pp. 218-22.

CHAPTER VII

JOHN HENRY BALLADS

THE EXACT time, place, and manner of origin of the ballad *John Henry* will probably never be known. Some sort of song has probably been sung about the steel driver ever since he won favor among his associates. Some of my informants say they heard *John Henry* in the early eighties. If John Henry did something to win fame at Big Bend Tunnel in 1870, 1871, or 1872, then it was evidently not long before his name was being sung.

After a short study of *John Henry* ballads I developed the hypothesis that there have been one or more printed versions of the ballad circulating. The rather formal style and structure of the ballads, standing as they do in contrast to the usual run of Negro songs, led me to this conclusion. Accordingly, I ran a brief "want ad" in five selected Negro newspapers in Virginia, West Virginia, Georgia, Kentucky, and Ohio. Through this advertisement I obtained an old printed *John Henry* from Mrs. C. L. Lynn, of Rome, Georgia. A photostatic reproduction appears in the frontispiece. The ballad bears the title, *John Henry, The Steel Driving Man*. It is printed on a sheet 4⅞ inches x 8½ inches. At the bottom is the name of the author, W. T. Blankenship, but no date is shown. Mrs. Lynn could tell me nothing as to the age of the ballad except that "it is a very old song, it has been in our family for years." Mr. W. G. Lownds, of the Mergenthaler Linotype Company, Brooklyn, New York, examined a photostat of the ballad and stated that he could not estimate the year in which it was printed, but he was certain that the type is hand composition. This does not permit us to set up an estimate on the age of the ballad, however. Mr. Henry Lewis Bullen, of the Typographic Library and Museum, Jersey City, New Jersey, also examined the ballad. He said, "The heading to the verses is set in type we now call 24-pt. Gothic Extra Condensed, No. 2, which was first made in 1862. . . . The type used in the text lines is much earlier." That is, the kind of type used in the ballad was in use before the ballad could possibly have originated and is still used to some extent. Therefore, there is no definitive typographical clue as to age to be found in the ballad.

However, it is practically certain that this is not the original version of *John Henry*. It appears to be a sort of composite version. Blankenship probably utilized several verses which were already current, adding a few of his own composition, to make this ballad. I entertain the belief that there is still another printed version which appeared earlier than Blankenship's and which is the original *John Henry* or is based upon the original. I cannot prove this, but I believe that in time someone will turn up one of these old prints.

Theoretically, I should outline the evolution of *John Henry* as follows: The first songs about John Henry were simple, spontaneous hammer songs which did not go into the details of the John Henry story. Perhaps here and there someone made up a brief song of the ballad type. A short time later some person who was familiar with the tradition composed a ballad and had it printed on single sheets for distribution at a low price, say five or ten cents. This was circulated in West Virginia and a few other states and was taken by the Negro laborers to various parts of the country. No copy of this hypothetical ballad has yet been found. Still later, one or more persons wrote and printed different versions of the ballad and sold them. One such version, that written by Blankenship, has come to light. It was probably published about 1900 or a little earlier and the author was probably a white man.[1] Which of his stanzas were new and which borrowed cannot be told, however, because of our lack of knowledge as to the possible versions of *John Henry* antedating his.

If the original *John Henry* was a folk version in the purest sense, it probably was composed of a few simple stanzas which grew by gradual accretion. If it was written by one person, it was more likely to have had eight or ten stanzas or even more. The rather formal nature of the ballad as it is known today suggests that, even if the original was a pure folk product, it was taken over early in its existence by some ballad-maker and set into a mold which it has followed pretty closely up to the present.

The number of separate stanzas in the different versions of *John Henry* is not exceedingly large, but the variations within a given stanza and the arrangement of stanzas in a given version are almost infinite. Take, for example, the common variations of the usual opening stanza:

> John Henry was a little boy
> Sittin' on his papa's knee,
> Said, "The Big Bend Tunnel on the C. & O. Road
> Is goin' to be the death of me,
> Is goin' to be the death of me."

John may be *a little babe, a little man, just three weeks old,* etc. He may be sitting on his *mammy's,* or *mother's,* or *father's* knee. His premonition may be for the *Tunnel No. Nine, a big high tower, a big wheel turnin',*[2] or half a dozen other

---

[1] Professor Collier Cobb, University of North Carolina, tells me that he recalls having seen a *John Henry* ballad by Blankenship about 1900. He also says that in collecting folk songs he came across Blankenship productions several times, and he is fairly certain that this author was a white man.

[2] A corruption of Big Bend Tunnel. A common dialect pronunciation of "tunnel" is "turnel."

things, and these may be on the *B. & O. Road,* the *N. & W. Road,* the *Air Line Road* or any other familiar to the singer. Many of the stanzas are capable of the same sort of variation as this one.

It is only natural, of course, that many of the stanzas have strayed far from the original simple story of John Henry, some being entirely irrelevant. Virtually every *John Henry* version known has one or more stanzas about John Henry's wife or woman. Some of these are no doubt derived from certain stanzas in *The Lass of Roch Royal,* an old English ballad which is still sung in the Appalachians. Others have been composed from time to time by appreciative singers who realized that the tragedy of John Henry was not complete without the spectacle of his woman mourning for him.

The ballads which follow are not given in any particularly logical order, except that in a general way they progress from the more finished or coherent versions toward the fragmentary and corrupt versions. It is futile to attempt to classify *John Henry* ballads according to conventional methods, for many of the variants are composed of stanzas portraying disconnected scenes. The stanza, not the song, is the unit. A *John Henry* ballad is likely to be composed of any combination of stanzas, and often the narrative is none too clear. Such notes as are relevant are presented in connection with the songs. Several tunes are given. I have tried in every possible way to obtain the tune of every song, but it is almost impossible to get tunes when the collector does not hear the contributor sing his song. In only one instance was I successful in getting a tune by mail. I have included several phonograph record versions because they are remarkably good reproductions of folk singing. The various record manufacturers generously granted permission to quote their records.

The dialect in the ballads is not consistent. Dialect is not consistent in actual usage, and there is no point in attempting to make all of the songs conform to some imaginary mode or average. Those versions which my informants have written for me I have faithfully reproduced, and I disclaim any responsibility for the dialect therein.

The phonograph and radio[3] versions of *John Henry* which have come out within the past two years are giving the ballad a new birth among Negroes and are introducing it to thousands of white people who have never heard it before. They are also complicating the field work for the person who collects *John Henry* ballads in the future. Fortunately nearly all of my collecting was done before the phonograph ballads began circulating, and I have had no difficulty in detecting the relationships of the phonograph versions and my versions where such relationships exist. After a few years, however, numerous queer offsprings of the liaison between phonographic and folk productions[4] will arise to confound the collector.

I

This is the Blankenship printed version of *John Henry* obtained from Mrs. C. L. Lynn, of Rome, Georgia. I reproduce it here because the photostat is difficult to read in places. Unfortunately I could not get the tune of this version. Note that the usual opening stanza about John Henry's sitting on his

[3] I have heard of several radio productions of *John Henry*, but I have never managed to catch one; hence I have quoted none in this book.

[4] The *John Henry* records are all, I believe, authentic folk versions, but in a sense they cease to be real folk songs when they are put on phonograph records. The folk setting is lost, and the normal mode of folk song diffusion is upset. For a discussion of the interrelations between formal and folk productions, see the chapter on "Blues" in *Negro Workaday Songs*. See also my article, "Double Meanings in the Popular Negro Blues," *Journal of Abnormal and Social Psychology*, April, 1927.

mammy's knee is not here, although it was probably in existence long before Blankenship's broadside came out.

JOHN HENRY, THE STEEL DRIVING MAN

1. John Henry was a railroad man,
   He worked from six 'till five,
   "Raise 'em up bullies and let 'em drop down,
   I'll beat you to the bottom or die."

2. John Henry said to his captain:
   "You are nothing but a common man,
   Before that steam drill shall beat me down,
   I'll die with my hammer in my hand."

3. John Henry said to the Shakers:
   "You must listen to my call,
   Before that steam drill shall beat me down,
   I'll jar these mountains till they fall."

4. John Henry's captain said to him:
   "I believe these mountains are caving in."
   John Henry said to his captain: "Oh Lord!"
   "That's my hammer you hear in the wind."

5. John Henry he said to his captain:
   "Your money is getting mighty slim,
   When I hammer through this old mountain,
   Oh Captain will you walk in?"

6. John Henry's captain came to him
   With fifty dollars in his hand,
   He laid his hand on his shoulder and said:
   "This belongs to a steel driving man."

7. John Henry was hammering on the right side,
   The big steam drill on the left,
   Before that steam drill could beat him down,
   He hammered his fool self to death.

8. They carried John Henry to the mountains,
   From his shoulder his hammer would ring,
   She caught on fire by a little blue blaze
   I believe these old mountains are caving in.

9. John Henry was lying on his death bed,
   He turned over on his side,
   And these were the last words John Henry said
   "Bring me a cool drink of water before I die."

10. John Henry had a little woman,
    Her name was Pollie Ann,
    He hugged and kissed her just before he died,
    Saying, "Pollie, do the very best you can."

11. John Henry's woman heard he was dead,
    She could not rest on her bed,
    She got up at midnight, caught that No. 4 train,
    "I am going where John Henry fell dead."

12. They carried John Henry to that new burying ground
    His wife all dressed in blue,
    She laid her hand on John Henry's cold face,
    "John Henry I've been true to you."

Price 5 Cents   W. T. BLANKENSHIP

II

An unusual version is contributed by Leon R. Harris, of
Moline, Illinois, who has been interested in John Henry
for a long time. "I have been a 'Rambler' all my life," he
writes. "Ever since I ran away from the 'white folks' when
twelve years old,—and I have worked with my people in railroad grading camps from the Great Lakes to Florida and from
the Atlantic to the Missouri River, and, wherever I have
worked, I have always found someone who could and would
sing of John Henry. . . . This version of the song is the Virginia and West Virginia Version. Every verse, except per-

haps the 8th, 9th, and 16th, I have heard sung in the extra gangs and construction gangs that work along the C. & O. and N. & W. and their branches. If I remember correctly, I first heard the song in 1904, while employed by the contractor who built the Birmingham Powder Co.'s plant at Birmingham, Ala. I first heard the enclosed verses in 1909-10-11. The song is sung to many an air or tune, and hardly any two singers sing it alike. I have never seen any of these verses in print."

Mr. Harris is typical of a large number of "ramblers" who have worked all over the country and have scattered *John Henry* to the four corners of the nation. He was good enough to get the tune of his version noted for me. I give his song just as he wrote it, dialect and all. Note that, with exception of two lines in the twentieth stanza, this song has nothing in common with the Blankenship version. In fact, while it tells the same story as most of the other versions, it stands apart from all the others in its mode of expression.

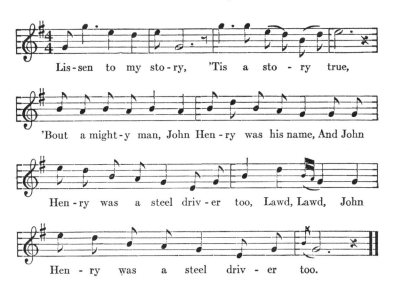

Lis-sen to my sto-ry, 'Tis a sto-ry true,

'Bout a might-y man, John Hen-ry was his name, And John

Hen-ry was a steel driv-er too, Lawd, Lawd, John

Hen-ry was a steel driv-er too.

1. Lissen to my story;
   'Tis a story true;
   'Bout a mighty man,—John Henry was his name,
   An' John Henry was a steel-driver too—
   Lawd,—Lawd,—
   John Henry was a steel-driver too.

2. John Henry had a hammah;
   Weighed nigh fo'ty poun';
   Eb'ry time John made a strike
   He seen his steel go 'bout two inches down,—
   Lawd,—Lawd,—
   He seen his steel go 'bout two inches down.

3. John Henry's woman, Lucy,—
   Dress she wore was blue;
   Eyes like stars an' teeth lak-a marble stone,
   An' John Henry named his hammah "Lucy" too,—
   Lawd,—Lawd,—
   John Henry named his hammah "Lucy" too.

4. Lucy came to see him;
   Bucket in huh han';
   All th' time John Henry ate his snack,
   O Lucy she'd drive steel lak-a man,—
   Lawd,—Lawd,—
   O Lucy she'd drive steel lak-a man.

5. John Henry's cap'n Tommy,—
   V'ginny gave him birth;
   Loved John Henry like his only son,
   And Cap' Tommy was the whitest man on earth,—
   Lawd,—Lawd,—
   Cap' Tommy was th' whitest man on earth.

6. One day Cap' Tommy told him
   How he'd bet a man;
   Bet John Henry'd beat a steam-drill down,
   Jes' cause he was th' best in th' lan',—
   Lawd,—Lawd,—
   'Cause he was th' best in th' lan'.

7. John Henry tol' Cap' Tommy;
   Lightnin' in his eye;
   "Cap'n, bet yo' las' red cent on me,
   Fo' I'll beat it to th' bottom or I'll die,—
   Lawd,—Lawd,—
   I'll beat it to th' bottom or I'll die."

8. "Co'n pone's in my stomach;
   Hammah's in my han';
   Haint no steam-drill on dis railroad job
   Can beat 'Lucy' an' her steel-drivin' man,
   Lawd,—Lawd,—
   Can beat 'Lucy' an' her steel-drivin' man."

9. "Bells ring on de engines;
   Runnin' down th' line;
   Dinnahs done when Lucy pulls th' c'od;
   But no hammah in this mountain rings like mine,—
   Lawd,—Lawd,—
   No hammah in this mountain rings like mine."

10. Sun shined hot an' burnin'
    Wer'n't no breeze at-tall;
    Sweat ran down like watah down a hill
    That day John Henry let his hammah fall,—
    Lawd,—Lawd,—
    That day John Henry let his hammah fall.

11. John Henry kissed his hammah;
    White Man turned on steam;
    Li'l Bill held John Henry's trusty steel,—
    'Twas th' biggest race th' worl' had ever seen,—
    Lawd,—Lawd,—
    Th' biggest race th' worl' had ever seen.

12. White Man tol' John Henry,—
    "Niggah, dam yo' soul,
    You might beat dis steam an' drill o' mine
    When th' rocks in this mountain turn to gol',—
    Lawd,—Lawd,—
    When th' rocks in this mountain turn to gol'."

13. John Henry tol' th' white man;
    Tol' him kind-a sad:
    "Cap'n George I want-a be yo' fr'en;
    If I beat yo' to th' bottom, don't git mad,—
    Lawd,—Lawd,—
    If I beat yo' to th' bottom don't git mad."

14. Cap' Tommy sees John Henry's
    Steel a-bitin' in;
    Cap'n slaps John Henry on th' back,
    Says, "I'll give yo' fifty dollars if yo' win,—
    Lawd,—Lawd,—
    I'll give yo' fifty dollars if yo' win."

15. White Man saw John Henry's
    Steel a-goin' down;
    White Man says,—"That man's a mighty man,
    But he'll weaken when th' hardes' rock is foun',—
    Lawd,—Lawd,—
    He'll weaken when th' hardes' rock is foun'."

16. John Henry, O John Henry,—
    John Henry's hammah too;
    When a woman's 'pendin' on a man
    Haint no tellin' what a mighty man can do,—
    Lawd,—Lawd,—
    No tellin' what a mighty man can do.

17. John Henry, O, John Henry!
    Blood am runnin' red!
    Falls right down with his hammah to th' groun',
    Says, "I've beat him to th' bottom but I'm dead,—
    Lawd,—Lawd,—
    I've beat him to th' bottom but I'm dead."

18. John Henry kissed his hammah;
    Kissed it with a groan;
    Sighed a sigh an' closed his weary eyes,
    Now po' Lucy has no man to call huh own,—
    Lawd,—Lawd,—
    Po' Lucy has no man to call huh own.

19. Cap' Tommy came a-runnin'
    To John Henry's side;
    Says, "Lawd, Lawd,—O Lawdy, Lawdy, Lawd,—
    He's beat it to th' bottom but he's died,—
    Lawd,—Lawd,—
    He's beat it to th' bottom but he's died."

20. Lucy ran to see him;
    Dress she wore was blue;
    Started down th' track an' she nevvah did turn back,
    Sayin', "John Henry, I'll be true—true to you,—
    Lawd,—Lawd,—
    John Henry, I'll be true—true to you."

21. John Henry, O, John Henry!
    Sing it if yo' can,—
    High an' low an' ev'ry where yo' go,—
    He died with his hammah in his han',—
    Lawd,—Lawd,—
    He died with his hammah in his han'.

22. Buddie, where'd yo' come from
    To this railroad job?
    If yo' wantta be a good steel-drivin' man,
    Put yo' trus' in yo' hammah an' yo' God,—
    Lawd,—Lawd,—
    Put yo' trus' in yo' hammah an' yo' God.

III

This lengthy version was sent in by Mr. Onah L. Spencer, of Cincinnati, Ohio. I take it that he has woven together his own arrangement of all the John Henry stanzas he has ever heard. Some of his stanzas I have never seen in any other version. Mr. Spencer writes in an unpublished manuscript to which he kindly gave me access: "I lived for twenty-five years on Baptist Hill (a Negro village in Cumminsville) Cincinnati, Ohio, in the environment of the illiterate of the race, in the cult of blues when jazz was in its babyhood. . . . In a neighborhood where rent was cheap, railroad construction employees, teamsters, and laborers from contracting jobs made their Mecca. Most of these men were new arrivals from the South. And in the evenings after supper was over, Bull Durham cigarettes were rolled and lighted and evening yarns would start their rounds. Most of these were folk tales. . . . And after the rusty bucket had made its 'umteenth' trip to the corner saloon, someone would suggest music, which consisted of a guitar to lead and another to second." John Henry, says Mr. Spencer, "usually initiated the new help to the spirit of the job, for if there was a slacker in a gang of workers it would stimulate him with its heroic masculine appeal." Here is the song just as Mr. Spencer wrote it out.

1. Some say he's from Georgia,
   Some say he's from Alabam,
   But it's wrote on the rock at the Big Ben Tunnel,
   That he's an East Virginia Man,
   That he's an East Virginia man.

2. John Henry was a steel drivin' man,
   He died with a hammah in his han',
   Oh, come along boys and line the track
   For John Henry ain't never comin' back,
   For John Henry ain't never comin' back.

3. John Henry he could hammah,
   He could whistle, he could sing,
   He went to the mountain early in the mornin'
   To hear his hammah ring,
   To hear his hammah ring.

4. John Henry went to the section boss,
   Says the section boss what kin you do?
   Says I can line a track, I kin histe a jack,
   I kin pick and shovel too,
   I kin pick and shovel too.

5. John Henry told the cap'n,
   When you go to town,
   Buy me a nine pound hammah
   An' I'll drive this steel drill down,
   An' I'll drive this steel drill down.

6. Cap'n said to John Henry,
   You've got a willin' mind.
   But you just well lay yoh hammah down,
   You'll nevah beat this drill of mine,
   You'll nevah beat this drill of mine.

7. John Henry went to the tunnel
   And they put him in lead to drive,
   The rock was so tall and John Henry so small
   That he laid down his hammah and he cried,
   That he laid down his hammah and he cried.

8. The steam drill was on the right han' side,
   John Henry was on the left,
   Says before I let this steam drill beat me down,
   I'll hammah myself to death,
   I'll hammah myself to death.

9. Oh the cap'n said to John Henry,
   I bleeve this mountain's sinkin' in.
   John Henry said to the cap'n, Oh my!
   Tain't nothin' but my hammah suckin' wind,
   Tain't nothin' but my hammah suckin' wind.

10. John Henry had a cute liddle wife,
    And her name was Julie Ann,
    And she walk down the track and nevah look back,
    Goin' to see her brave steel drivin' man,
    Goin' to see her brave steel drivin' man.

11. John Henry had a pretty liddle wife,
    She come all dressed in blue.
    And the last words she said to him,
    John Henry I been true to you,
    John Henry I been true to you.

12. John Henry was on the mountain,
    The mountain was so high,
    He called to his pretty liddle wife,
    Said Ah kin almos' touch the sky,
    Said Ah kin almos' touch the sky.

13. Who gonna shoe yoh pretty liddle feet,
    Who gonna glove yoh han',
    Who gonna kiss yoh rosy cheeks,
    An' who gonna be yoh man,
    An' who gonna be yoh man?

14. Papa gonna shoe my pretty liddle feet,
    Mama gonna glove my han',
    Sistah gonna kiss my rosy cheeks,
    An' I ain't gonna have no man,
    An' I ain't gonna have no man.

15. Then John Henry told huh,
    Don't you weep an' moan,
    I got ten thousand dollars in the First National Bank,
    I saved it to buy you a home,
    I saved it to buy you a home.

16. John Henry took his liddle boy,
    Sit him on his knee,
    Said that Big Ben Tunnel
    Gonna be the death of me,
    Gonna be the death of me.

17. John Henry took that liddle boy,
    Helt him in the pahm of his han',
    And the last words he said to that chile was,
    I want you to be a steel drivin' man,
    I want you to be a steel drivin' man.

18. John Henry ast that liddle boy,
    Now what are you gonna be?
    Says if I live and nothin' happen,
    A steel drivin' man I'll be,
    A steel drivin' man I'll be.

19. Then John Henry he did hammah,
    He did make his hammah soun',
    Says now one more lick fore quittin' time,
    An' I'll beat this steam drill down,
    An' I'll beat this steam drill down.

20. The hammah that John Henry swung,
    It weighed over nine poun',
    He broke a rib in his left han' side,
    And his intrels fell on the groun',
    And his intrels fell on the groun'.

21. All the women in the West
    That heard of John Henry's death,
    Stood in the rain, flagged the east bound train,
    Goin' where John Henry dropped dead,
    Goin' where John Henry dropped dead.

22. John Henry's liddle mother
    Was all dressed in red,
    She jumped in bed, covered up her head,
    Said I didn't know my boy was dead,
    Said I didn't know my boy was dead.

23. They took John Henry to the White House,
    And buried him in the san',
    And every locomotive come roarin' by,
    Says there lays that steel drivin' man,
    Says there lays that steel drivin' man.

IV

This was sung by Odell Walker, formerly of Chapel Hill. When he told the story of John Henry, he would speak of Big Bend Tunnel, but in the fourth stanza of his song he referred to "Big high tower on C. & O. Road." This version is rather abbreviated, but it contains the essential points in John Henry's history. It was obtained in 1925 and was published in *Negro Workaday Songs,* page 225.

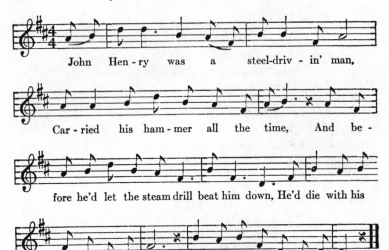

John   Hen - ry   was   a   steel-driv - in' man,

Car - ried   his ham - mer all   the   time,   And be -

fore he'd let the steam drill beat him down, He'd die with his

ham-mer in his hand , Die with his ham-mer in his hand.

1. John Henry was a steel-drivin' man,
   Carried his hammer all the time;
   And before he'd let the steam drill beat him down
   He'd die with his hammer in his hand,
   Die with his hammer in his hand.

2. John Henry went to the mountain,
   Beat that steam drill down;
   Rock was high, po' John was small,
   Well, he laid down his hammer an' he died,
   Laid down his hammer an' he died.

3. John Henry was a little babe
   Sittin' on his daddy's knee,
   Said, "Big high tower on C. & O. road
   Gonna be the death o' me,
   Gonna be the death o' me."

4. John Henry had a little girl,
   Her name was Polly Ann.
   John was on his bed so low,
   She drove with his hammer like a man,
   Drove with his hammer like a man.

V

Contributed by Edward Douglas, who is now staying for a while at the Ohio State Penitentiary: "I have succeeded in recalling and piecing together 13 verses," he says. "It was necessary to interview a number of Old-Timers of this Penitentiary to get some of the missing words and to verify my recolections." Mr. Douglas first heard about John Henry from his grandfather, who worked "on all the big jobs throughout the country, in them days, when steam drills were not so popular."

Some of the stanzas are apparently out of their proper places, but I leave them just as they were given to me. In this version the drilling contest is described and it is made clear that John Henry won. Several stanzas have near counterparts in Blankenship's ballad.

1. When John Henry was a little boy,
   Sitting upon his father's knee,
   His father said, "Look here, my boy,
   You must be a steel driving man like me,
   You must be a steel driving man like me."

2. John Henry went upon the mountain,
   Just to drive himself some steel.
   The rocks was so tall and John Henry so small,
   He said lay down hammer and squeal,
   He said lay down hammer and squeal.

3. John Henry had a little wife,
   And the dress she wore was red;
   The last thing before he died,
   He said, "Be true to me when I'm dead,
   Oh, be true to me when I'm dead."

4. John Henry's wife ask him for fifteen cents,
   And he said he didn't have but a dime,
   Said, "If you wait till the rising sun goes down,
   I'll borrow it from the man in the mine,
   I'll borrow it from the man in the mine."

5. John Henry started on the right-hand side,
   And the steam drill started on the left.
   He said, "Before I'd let that steam drill beat me down,
   I'd hammer my fool self to death,
   Oh, I'd hammer my fool self to death."

6. The steam drill started at half past six,
   John Henry started the same time.
   John Henry struck bottom at half past eight,
   And the steam drill didn't bottom till nine,
   Oh, the steam drill didn't bottom till nine.

7. John Henry said to his captain,
   "A man, he ain't nothing but a man,
   Before I'd let that steam drill beat me down,
   I'd die with the hammer in my hand,
   Oh, I'd die with the hammer in my hand."

8. John Henry said to his shaker,
   "Shaker, why don't you sing just a few more rounds?
   And before the setting sun goes down,
   You're gonna hear this hammer of mine sound,
   You're gonna hear this hammer of mine sound."

9. John Henry hammered on the mountain,
   He hammered till half past three,
   He said, "This big Bend Tunnel on the C. & O. road
   Is going to be the death of me,
   Lord! is going to be the death of me."

10. John Henry had a little baby boy,
    You could hold him in the palm of your hand.
    The last words before he died,
    "Son, you must be a steel driving man,
    Son, you must be a steel driving man."

11. John Henry had a little woman,
    And the dress she wore was red,
    She went down the railroad track and never come back,
    Said she was going where John Henry fell dead,
    Said she was going where John Henry fell dead.

12. John Henry hammering on the mountain
    As the whistle blew for half past two,
    The last word I heard him say,
    "Captain, I've hammered my insides in two,
    Lord, I've hammered my insides in two."

VI

Another man who had some difficulty with the law sent me
a *John Henry*. His name is J. D. Williams, and his address,
Kentucky Penitentiary, Eddyville, Kentucky, is good indefi-
nitely. His travels and his troubles, as he related them in
a short biography which he wrote for me, are suggestive of
Professor Odum's "Black Ulysses."

I have done a little punctuating and lining to make the
verses more readable; otherwise they stand as written. Except for an abbreviated opening stanza and an attack of
paramnesia in the eleventh, the stanzas fit fairly well into the
usual John Henry rhythm.

1. Ever body in the land
   Know John Henry was a steel driveing man,
   And knowed John Henry was a steel driveing man.

2. John Henry had a little baby,
   He'd sit him in the palm of his hand
   And all of his talk was to his baby son, "I want you to be
   a steel driveing man,
   And I want you to be a steel driveing man."

3. John Henry had a little woman,
   Her name was Paul E. Ann.[5]
   She could pick up a jack and lay down a track
   And hammer like a natural man,
   And hammer like a natural man.

4. "Paul E. Ann, who bought you these pretty little shoes?
   Who bought you the dress you wear so fine?
   And who kissed your red rosy cheeks?
   And whose going to be your man?"

5. "John Henry bought these pretty little shoes,
   John Henry bought the dress I wear so fine,
   John Henry kissed my red rosy cheeks,
   And you know I don't need no man."

6. John Henry, hammared in the mountains,
   It sounded like an earth quake in the ground.
   He said, "Don't go a way, no body,
   Just my hammer falling down,
   And just my hammar falling down."

7. John Henry told his Captain,
   "Go and tell your man they'd better run and pray,
   Because ever time my hammer falls,
   I feel the mountain giveing away."

8. John Henry sit down one day
   At dinner time to rest.
   His Captain walk up to him and said,
   "John Henry, I believe that steam hammer got you best."

9. John Henry told his Captain,
   "A man ain't nothing but a man.
   Before I'll let this steam hammer beat me down,
   I'll die with my hammer in my hand."

[5] A corruption of Polly Ann.

10. John Henry said to his Captain,
   "Captain, can't you see,
      Your hole is choked and your steel is broke
      And your hammer can't go down with me?"

11. Over five hundred people stood around,
   Just to see John Henry beat that steam hammer down.
   When John Henry beat that steam hammer down
   He stretched out on the ground and said to his friends
      around,
   "And I was the best, but I am going home to rest,
   That steam hammer is done broke me down."

12. When John Henry's little wife got the news
   That John Henry'd done fell dead,
      And the dress she ware was red,
   She walked down the C & O tracks and never look back,
   "I'm going to see where John Henry fell dead."

13. And when she got to where John Henry fell dead
   She fell down on her knees,
      And kissed him on the cheek, and these are the words she
      said,
   "Lord, there is one more good man done fell dead."

VII

This version is quoted by permission from Columbia Record, 15019-D, *John Henry*, sung by Gid Tanner and Riley Puckett. The record is excellently done, and the tune is typical. The same song with more noise from the accompanying instruments will be found on Columbia Record 15142-D.

John   Hen - ry   was   a   lit - tle   man,

Sittin' on   his   pa - pa's   knee,   Give   a   long   and loud and

lone - some   cry,   "The   ham-mer   be   the death   of

me,   pa - pa,   The ham-mer   be   the death   of   me."

1. John Henry was a little man,
    Sittin' on his papa's knee,
    Give a long and loud and lonesome cry,
  "The hammer be the death of me, papa,
    The hammer be the death of me."

2. John Henry told his captain,
    "Lawd, a man ain't nothin' but a man,
    But before I'll be driven by your old steam drill,
    Lawd, I'd die with the hammer in my hand," *etc.*

3. John Henry had a little hammer,
    Handle was made of bone,
    Every time he hit the steel on the head,
    Lawd it's . . . . [6]

[6] I am unable to understand this line. I wrote to the singers for help but received no reply.

4. John Henry walked in the tunnel,
   Had his captain by his side;
   But the rock so tall, John Henry so small,
   Lawd, he laid down his hammer and he cried, *etc.*

5. John Henry told his shaker,
   "Shaker, you better pray,
   If I miss this piece of steel,
   Tomorrow be your buryin' day, *etc.*

6. John Henry's captain sat on a rock,
   Says, "I believe my mountain's fallin' in."
   John Henry turned around and said,
   "It's my hammer fallin' in the wind," *etc.*

7. John Henry had a little woman,
   Her name was Polly Ann.
   John Henry lay sick down on his bed,
   Polly drove steel like a man, *etc.*

8. John Henry had just one only son,
   He could stand in the pa'm of your hand.
   Last words that John Henry said,
   "Son, don't be a steel-drivin' man," *etc.*

9. Took John Henry to the white house,
   Rolled him in the sand.
   The men from the east and the ladies from the west
   Came to see that good old steel-drivin' man, *etc.*

VIII

Mr. Melvin T. Hairston, of Raleigh, West Virginia, sends
this version. He is a firm believer in John Henry. "It was a
true story. . . . I was acquainted with one of his nephews and
have talked with one of the men that was turning the steel
for him." The drilling episode is not given much space in his
song, but it is at least a relief to see John Henry's woman with
some other name than Polly Ann.

1. John Henry, who was a baby
   Sitting on his papa's knee.
   He said, "The Big Ben Tunnel on the C. & O. Road,
   It is sure to be the death of me.
   It is sure to be the death of me."

   O shaker, huh turner, let her go down,
   O shaker, huh turner, let her go down.

2. They took John Henry from the big white house
   And they put him in the tunnel for to drive,
   With two nine-pound hammers hanging by his side
   And the steam drill pointing to the sky, *etc.*

   O shaker, huh turner, let her go down,
   O shaker, huh turner, let her go down.

3. John Henry was standing on the right hand side
   And the steam drill standing on the left.
   He said, "Before I would let you beat me down,
   I would hammer my fool self to death, *etc.*

   Oh, he died with his hammer in his hand,
   Oh, he died with his hammer in his hand.

4. John Henry, he had a woman,
   Her name was Mary Magdalene.
   She would go to the tunnel and sing for John,
   Just to hear John Henry's hammer ring, *etc.*

   Oh, he died with his hammer in his hand,
   Oh, he died with his hammer in his hand.

5. Well, they took John Henry to the new burying ground
   And they covered him up in the sand,
   And I see his little woman coming down the street,
   She says, "Yonder lay my steel-driving man," *etc.*

   Oh, he died with his hammer in his hand,
   Oh, he died with his hammer in his hand.

6. Some said he come from Kentucky,
   Some said he come from Spain.
   It was written on his tombstone and placed at his head,
   "John Henry was an East Virginia man," *etc.*

   Oh, he died with his hammer in his hand,
   Oh, he died with his hammer in his hand.

IX

A Tennessee version, collected by Professor Odum when he was attending the Scopes trial at Dayton; here, as in many other versions, it is not clear whether John Henry beat the steam drill or not. Stanzas 3, 6, 8, and 9 are related to Blankenship's version.

1. John Henry was a coal black man,
   Chicken chocolate brown;
   "Befo' I let your steamer get me down,
   I die wid my hammer in my han', Lawd, Lawd."

2. John Henry had a pretty little woman,
   She rode that Southbound train;
   She stopped in a mile of the station up there,
   "Let me hear John Henry's hammer ring, Lawd, Lawd."

3. John Henry sittin' on the left-han' side
   An' the steam drill on the right;
   The rock it was so large an' John Henry so small,
   He laid down his hammer an' he cried, "Lawd, Lawd."

4. John Henry had a pretty little woman,
   Her name was Julie Ann,
   She walked through the lan' with a hammer in her han',
   Sayin', "I drive steel like a man, Lawd, Lawd."

5. John Henry had a little woman,
   Her name was Julie Ann;
   John Henry took sick on his work one day,
   An' Julie Ann drove steel like a man, Lawd, Lawd.

6. John Henry had a pretty little boy,
   Sittin' in de palm of his han';
   He hugged an' kissed him an' bid him farewell,
   "O son, do the best you can, Lawd, Lawd."

7. John Henry was a little boy
   Sittin' on his papa's knee,
   Looked down at a big piece o' steel,
   Saying, "Papa, that'll be the death o' me, Lawd, Lawd."

8. John Henry had a pretty little woman,
   The dress she wore was red,
   She went down the track an' never did look back,
   Sayin', "I'm goin' where John Henry fell dead, Lawd, Lawd."

9. John Henry had a pretty little girl,
   The dress she wore was blue,
   She followed him to the graveyard sayin',
   "John Henry I've been true to you, Lawd, Lawd."

X

This version and the next belong together. They are a concrete example of the evolution of a ballad. The first was submitted by Miss Muriel Belton, a student at Southern University, Scotlandville, Louisiana. She learned it from hearing it sung by a Negro comedian named Jake, who traveled with a medicine seller known as Doctor Moon. First, however, the young lady sent her manuscript to her mother who lives at Dodson, Louisiana. Mrs. Belton not only forwarded her daughter's version, but sent also her own revision of it. She writes, "You will note slight changes in both the meter and the rhyme, also an original second stanza which prevents John Henry's going to the Mountain while still a baby." Version XI is Mrs. Belton's revision of X.

1. John Henry was a little baby
   Sittin' on his papa's knee.
   "Pa, I think I'll be a good steel driver,
   I will go to the mountain and see,
   O boy, I will go to the mountain and see."

2. John Henry went to the mountain,
   The mountain looked so tall,
   He laid his hammer by his side,
   Said, "A ten pound hammer is too small," *etc.*

3. John Henry said to the captain,
   "I'm nothing but a natural man.
   Before I'll let your steam drill beat me down,
   I will die with my hammer in my hand."

4. John Henry got a thirty pound hammer,
   Steam drill by his side,
   He drove that steam drill three inches
   And died with his hammer in his hand.

5. They carried him down by the river,
   Buried him in the sand,
   And every body that passed along
   Said, "There lies that steel driving man."

6. When the women in the West heard of John Henry's
      death,
   They couldn't lay still in their bed.
   Next morning they caught the east-bound train,
   Saying, "I'm going where John Henry fell dead."

XI

1. John Henry was a little baby,
   Sitting on his papa's knee;
   He said, "Pa, I think, when I get grown,
   A steel driving man I'll be, (O dad)
   A steel driving man I'll be."

2. John Henry said to his papa,
   "It's come my time to go;
   I'll get me a ten-pound hammer, dad,
   And go to the mountain, you know, (this day)
   I'll go to the mountain you know."

3. John Henry went to the mountain,
   The mountain looked so tall;
   He laid his hammer down by his side,
   Said, "A tenpounder is too small, (on the job)
   A ten pounder is too small."

4. John Henry said to the Captain,
   "I'm nothing but a natural man.
   Before I'll let your steam drill beat me
   I'll die with my hammer in my hand, (O boss)
   I'll die with my hammer in my hand."

5. John Henry got a thirty pound hammer,
   Beside the steam drill he did stand;
   He beat that steam drill three inches down
   And died with his hammer in his hand, (O boy)
   He died with his hammer in his hand.

6. They carried him down by the river,
   And buried him in the sand,
   And everybody that passed along,
   Said, "There lies that steel driving man, (So sad)
   There lies that steel driving man."

7. When the women in the West heard of John Henry's
       death,
   They couldn't lie still in their beds.
   Next morning they caught an east-bound train,
   Saying, "I'm going where John Henry fell dead! (Must
       go)
   I'm going where John Henry fell dead."

XII

Another good phonograph version, entitled *John Henry Blues,* is found on Okeh Record, 45101, performed by "Earl Johnson and His Dixie Entertainers." I reproduce it here by permission.

John Hen - ry was a lit - tle boy

Set - tin' on his pa - pa's knee. He

picked up a ham-mer and a piece of steel, Said,

"Cause the death of me, Cause the death of me."

1. John Henry was a little boy
   Settin' on his papa's knee.
   He picked up a hammer and a piece of steel,
   Said, "Cause the death of me,
   Cause the death of me."

2. John Henry went upon the mountain,
   Come down on the other side.
   Mountain was so tall, John Henry was so small,
   He throwed down his hammer and he cried, *etc.*

3. When they bought that new steam drill,
   They thought it was mighty fine.
   John Henry made his fourteen feet
   While the steam drill made only nine, *etc.*

4. John Henry said to his captain,
   "I ain't nothing but a man.
   Before I'll let the steam drill beat me down
   I'll die with my hammer in my hand," *etc.*

5. John Henry got sick and had to go home.
   This is what he said,
   "Fix me a place I want-a lay down,
   Got a mighty roaring in my head," *etc.*

6. John Henry had a little woman,
   Her name was Polly Ann.
   John Henry got sick and he had to go to bed,
   Polly drove steel like a man, *etc.*

7. "Where did you get them shoes you wear,
   The dresses that look so fine?"
   "Got my shoes from a railroad man,
   Dresses from a driver in the mine," *etc.*

XIII

In January and February, 1927, I held a John Henry contest among the County Training Schools in North Carolina. From the Moore County Training School, Carthage, came five entries which were practically identical. I went to Carthage and found that a group of students who had been singing *John Henry* had decided to submit their versions individually. The pupils admitted having heard one or more phonograph records of *John Henry* (Columbia and Okeh were mentioned) but their product is something different. Words and tune are both different, though related rather closely to the phonograph versions. Here is another good example of the process of transformation which a song undergoes in its folk journey.

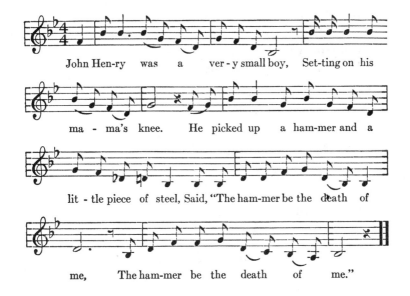

John Hen-ry was a ver-y small boy, Set-ting on his ma-ma's knee. He picked up a ham-mer and a lit-tle piece of steel, Said, "The ham-mer be the death of me, The ham-mer be the death of me."

1. John Henry was a very small boy
   Setting on his mama's knee.
   He picked up a hammer and a little piece of steel,
   Said, "The hammer be the death of me,
   The hammer be the death of me."

2. John Henry went upon the mountain,
   Came down on the other side.
   The mountain was so tall, John Henry was so small,
   He laid down his hammer and he cried, "O Lord." *etc.*

3. John Henry on the right hand side,
   The steam drill on the left,
   "Before I'll let your steam drill beat me down,
   I'm gonna hammer my fool self to death."

4. "Oh, look away over yonder, captain,
   You can't see like me."
   He hollered out in a lonesome cry,
   "A hammer be the death of me."

5. John Henry told the captain,
    "When you go to town,
        Bring me back a twelve-pound hammer,
        I will sho' beat your steam drill down."

6. The man that invented the steam drill
    Thought he was mighty fine.
        John Henry drove his fourteen feet
        And the steam drill only made nine.

7. John Henry told his shaker,
    "Shaker, you better pray,
        For, if I miss the six-foot steel,
        Tomorrow'll be your burying day."

8. John Henry had a pretty little wife,
    Her name was Mary Ann.
        He said, "Fix me a place to lay down, child,
        I got a roaring in my head."

9. John Henry had a loving little wife,
    The dress she wore was blue.
        She walked down the track but never came back,
        "John Henry, I've been true to you."

10. John Henry told the captain
     Just before he died,
        "Only one favor I ask of you:
        Take care of my wife and child."

XIV

Still another phonograph version of *John Henry* is found on Brunswick Record, 112-A, *Death of John Henry*, sung by Uncle Dave Macon. Uncle Dave's mellow voice and his banjo accompaniment make a very pleasing effect.

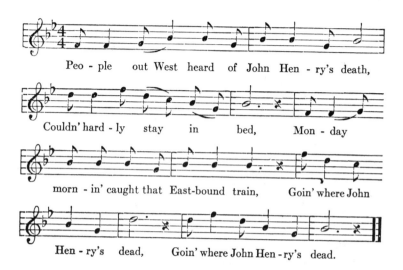

Peo - ple out West heard of John Hen - ry's death,
Couldn' hard - ly stay in bed, Mon - day
morn - in' caught that East-bound train, Goin' where John
Hen - ry's dead, Goin' where John Hen - ry's dead.

1. People out West heard of John Henry's death,
   Couldn' hardly stay in bed,
   Monday mornin' caught that East-bound train,
   Goin' where John Henry's dead,
   Goin' where John Henry's dead.

2. Carried John Henry to the grave yard
   And looked at him good and long.
   Very last words his wife said to him,
   "My husband, he is dead and gone,
   My husband, he is dead and gone."

3. John Henry's wife wore a brand new dress,
   It was all trimmed in blue.
   Very last words she said to him,
   "Honey, I've been true to you," *etc.*

4. John Henry told the shaker,
   "Lordy, shake while I sing.
   Pulling a hammer from my shoulder,
   I'm bound to hear her when she rings," *etc.*

5. John Henry told his captain,
   "I am a Tennessee man.
   Before I would see that steam drill beat me down,
   Die with my hammer in my hand," *etc.*

6. John Henry hammered in the mountains
   Till the hammer caught on fire.
   Very last words I heard him say,
   "Cool drink of water 'fore I die," *etc.*

XV

This was contributed by W. A. Bates, Cleveland, Ohio. He admitted that he was not fully satisfied with the form of his version, but—"I am a busy race man from morn till night. I am now writing a mighty play entitled 'Tears of Regret,' but my typewriter has struck on account it needs more blue ribbon and lighter fingers on the keys."

1. John Henry was man who everyone knew,
   His mighty pile-driving none ever knew
   Till that hot summer day he died,
   There was his mother and many others who cried.

2. John Henry had a little wife
   By the name of Polly Ann.
   John Henry got sick and had to go to bed,
   Polly Ann drove steel like a man, buddy,
   She drove steel like a natural man.

3. John Henry was as strong as could be,
   But he says, "The Big Bend Tunnel on the C. & O. Road
   Is going to be the death of me."

4. "Captain, captain, O captain,
   You oughter be ashame,
   You have called the pay roll
   And never called my name."

5. John Henry had a little son,
   You could put him in the palm of your hand.
   He said, "That's all right, anyhow,
   My daddy is a steel-driving man, buddy,
   My daddy is a steel-driving man."

6. His fists was of steel, his heart was of stone.
   When he rung his hammer
   'Twas slight of hand and bacon at home.[7]

7. John Henry drove a spike up near the crown.
   John Henry laughed when the boys all laughed,,
   Said, "It's nothing but my hammer falling down."

8. John Henry had a little wife
   Who were steel corn fed.
   She went down the track and never looked back,
   "Lord, I'm going where my man fell dead."

XVI

The contributor of this is a young man of Rocky Mount, Virginia. He writes: "On hearing that you are making a special study of John Henry, and want to publish his songs when you have them collected in one volume; I as a member of the 'Negro Race,' will be glad to give you any information that will help do anything for the uplift of my race. On page three you will find the story in song of that great steel driver who beat the steam drill! . . . I learned it from my father. It is at least 50 years old. . . . Let me hear from you at once. John Turnbull."

1. John Henry was a little lad,
   Sitting on his father's knee,
   O! the Big Ben Tunnel on the C. & O. road,
   Is going to be your death I mean, Ho-de-loo,
   Going to be your death I mean.

[7] A corrupt line.

2. John Henry said to the captain,
   "A man ain't nothing but a man.
   And before I'll be governed by this old steam drill,
   Lawd, I'll die with the hammer in my hand, Ho-de-loo,
   Law I'll die with the hammer in my hand."

3. John Henry had a little gal,
   Her name was Poly Ann,
   John Henry was sick and in the bed,
   Poly drove steel like a man, Ho-de-loo,
   Poly drove steel like a man.

XVII

Mr. Walter H. Jordan, of New York City, a man of considerable experience in steel driving, has written me frequently about John Henry. In one of his letters he says: "Very often in camp, years ago, I have heard the men swear that they could still hear the ghosts of old hammer men driving steel in Big Ben. I have heard them with their banjos sing of John Henry, improvise perhaps thirty or forty verses. . . . After twenty-five or thirty years—it has been that long since I have seen any work done with a hammer—the only verses of John Henry I can remember are these." Mr. Jordan, I might add, does not put much faith in the John Henry legend. If the truth could be found, he says, "another good Negro myth would be exploded."

1. . . . .
   . . . .
   Oh, the Big Bend Tunnel on the C. & O. Road
   Laid John Henry so low,
   Laid John Henry so low.

2. The contractor got uneasy,
   Thought the tunnel was coming in.
   But John Henry cried out with a very loud shout,
   "It's nothin' but my hammer when she rings,
   It's nothin' but my hammer when she rings."

3. John Henry had a little woman,
   She come all dressed in blue.
   This is what she said when she found he was dead,
   "Oh, John Henry, I've been true to you,
   Oh, John Henry, I've been true to you."

4. Some said he came from England,
   Some said he came from Spain.
   But it's no such a thing, he was an east Virginia man
   And he died with his hammer in his hand,
   And he died with his hammer in his hand.

XVIII

The next two are from St. Helena Island, South Carolina.
I had brought four men together to sing spirituals and found
that two could sing *John Henry*. The singers had some discussion as to how *John Henry* ought to be sung; so they finally
decided that each should sing it as he pleased. The first was
sung by Thomas Watkins, the second by Richard Sheadrack.

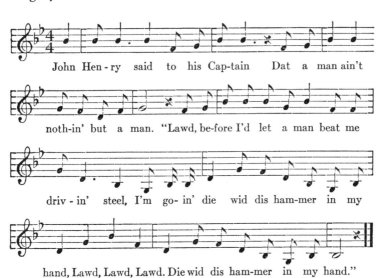

John Hen-ry said to his Cap-tain Dat a man ain't
noth-in' but a man. "Lawd, be-fore I'd let a man beat me
driv-in' steel, I'm go-in' die wid dis ham-mer in my
hand, Lawd, Lawd, Lawd. Die wid dis ham-mer in my hand."

1. John Henry said to his Captain
   Dat a man ain't nothin' but a man.
   "Lawd, before I'd let a man beat me drivin' steel,
   I'm goin' die wid dis hammer in my hand, Lawd, Lawd,
       Lawd,
   Die wid dis hammer in my hand."

2. When John Henry was a little boy
   He sit down on his father's knee.
   He p'int his hand at a piece of steel,
   Said, "Dat goin' be the death of me, Lawd, Lawd, Lawd,
   Dat goin' be the death of me."

3. John Henry said to his captain,
   "Captain, w'en you go to town,
   Won't you bring me back a nine-pound hammer, my
       captain?
   I'm goin' drive dis steel on down, Lawd, Lawd, Lawd,
   Drive dis steel on down."

4. John Henry went upon the mountain,
   Had a hundred and forty men.
   W'en de sun commence to shine and de steam fall down,
   Leave no one to drive but him, Lawd, Lawd, Lawd,
   No one to drive but him.

5. He said, "Weh get your shoes, little woman,
   And your dress all trimmed so fine?"
   "Lawd, I get my shoes from a railroad man,
   I get my dress from a driver in de mine, Lawd, Lawd,
       Lawd,
   Dress from a driver in de mine."

6. Said, "Weh you goin' now, little woman,
   Wid your dress all trimmed in red?"
   Said, "I'm goin' right down to the railroad track,
   Weh my husband John Henry fell dead, Lawd, Lawd,
       Lawd,
   My husband John Henry fell dead."

XIX

John Hen-ry was a lit-tle boy, And he set on his fa-ther's knee, Said, "Be-fore I'd let this drive me down, Lawd, I'm goin' die wid dis ham-mer in my hand, I'm goin' die wid de ham-mer in my hand."

1. John Henry was a little boy,
   And he set on his father's knee
   Said, "Before I'd let this drive me down,
   Lawd, I'm goin' die wid de hammer in my hand,
   I'm goin' die wid de hammer in my hand."

2. John Henry said to his captain,
   "Captain, w'en you go to town,
   Won't you bring me back a nine-pound hammer?
   I'm goin' drive dis steel on down,
   I'm goin' drive dis steel on down."

3. Oh, w'en I want good whiskey,
   Oh, w'en I want good corn,
   Baby, w'en I sing dat lonesome song,
   Honey, down de road I am gone,
   Honey, down de road I am gone.

4. John Henry had a little woman,
   And de dress she wear was red
   And she got her dress from a railroad man
   Got her shoes from a man in de mine,
   Got her shoes from a man in de mine.

5. John Henry had a little woman,
   And de dress she wear was red
   And she went down de road and she never looked back,
   "I am goin' weh my man fall dead,
   I am goin' weh my man fall dead."

6. John Henry had a little woman,
   And de dress she wear was red,
   Says, "If I miss my railroad time
   I'm goin' die wid de hammer in my hand,
   I'm goin' drive steel just like a man."

XX

This was sent to Professor Odum by William G. Parmenter, Miami, Florida, who learned it in the summer of 1920 while working on a gang near Jacksonville.

1. John Henry told the captain,
   "Captain, captain, gimme my time!
   I can make mo' money on the A. C. and L.
   Than I can on the Georgia Line."

2. John Henry told the captain,
   "Captain, when you go to town,
   Bring me back a ten-pound hammer,
   I's gonna knock this mountain down."

3. John Henry had a little woman,
   Just as pretty as she could be;
   They's just one objection I's got to her:
   She want every man she see.

4. John Henry asked his little woman,
   "Where you get those clothes and shoes so fine?"
   "Oh, I got the clothes from a railroad man
   And the shoes from a man in the mines."

XXI

From Maude Culbreth, Bluffton, Georgia, comes this condensed version. She writes, "I have been knowing the song of John Henry for 3 years. . . . I don't know exactly how old it is or when it was started up, but my folks have been knowing it for about 50 years."

1. John Henry told his captain,
   "A man ain't nothing but a man,
   And before I'd let this steel go down,
   I'd die with the hammer in my hand,
   I'd die with the hammer in my hand."

2. John Henry told his captain,
   "If you go to town today or tomorrow,
   Bring me back a ten pound hammer,
   I'm going to drive this steel on down,
   I'm going to drive this steel on down."

3. John Henry had a little wife,
   The hat she wore was red,
   The sweetest word she ever said,
   Was, "I'm going where Henry fell dead,
   I'm going where Henry fell dead."

4. John Henry had a little baby,
   You could hold him in the pa'm of your hand,
   And every time that baby cried,
   I'm going where Henry died.

XXII

Robert Mason, of Durham, North Carolina, is one of those "natural-born musicianers" who can make his twelve-string box "talk" *John Henry*. As his singing partner, Odell Walker, said, "He can pick that box in more ways than a farmer can whip a mule." Printed words and music are a poor substitute for such performance, but I give his song as one more variant in a long chain of John Henriana. This one begins as usual, but toward the end there is some detail about John Henry's domestic troubles.

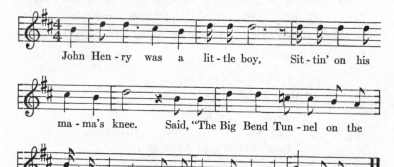

John Hen-ry was a lit-tle boy, Sit-tin' on his ma-ma's knee. Said, "The Big Bend Tun-nel on the C. and O. Road Gon-na cause the death of me, Lawd, Lawd."

1. John Henry was a little boy
   Sittin' on his mama's knee.
   Said, "The Big Bend Tunnel on the C. & O. Road
   Gonna cause the death of me, Lawd, Lawd."

2. John Henry told his captain,
   "A man ain't nothing but a man.
   Before I'd let you beat me down,
   I'd die with the hammer in my hand."

3. John Henry went to the tunnel,
   Thought he would make it very well,
   But when he came to realize,
   That big tower gave him hell.

4. "Where did you get your pretty little dress?
   The hat you wear so fine?"
   "Got my dress from a railroad man,
   Hat from a man in the mine."

5. Mother run to the window,
   Sister run to the do',
   Hollerin' an' screamin', Lawd, an' a-cryin',
   "John Henry, don't you go, Lawd, Lawd."

6. John Henry told his woman,
   "It's true I would carry you,
      But the work is hard and the camp is rough,
      There's nothing there you can do."

7. John Henry told his woman,
   "I've always did as I please."
      She said, "If you go with that other bitch,
      I will not let you see no ease."

XXIII

Ethel Marie Grays, a student at Virginia Normal and Industrial Institute, Petersburg, sent this. She learned it from her brother, who learned it while working on a railroad at Matoka, West Virginia, in 1919. The last stanza is common in railroad songs but does not belong to *John Henry*. Miss Grays says, "It is one which I thought contradicted the others, but I am adding it."

1. John Henry was a poor little boy
   Sitting on his father's knee.
      He said, "The Big Ben Tunnel on the C and O
      Going to be the death of me."

2. John Henry called his father,
   Said, "Father come and see."
      He pointed his hand at a piece of steel,
      Said, "It's going to be the death of me."

3. John Henry told his father,
   "Oh, father, this is my plan.
      If I live and don't die,
      I am going to be a steel driving man."

4. John Henry said to his father,
   "How do you like my plan?
      If I ever get on the C and O line
      I'm going to die with the hammer in my hand."

5. John Henry had a pretty little wife,
   He said, "Come sit on my knee.
   You have been the death of a many poor man,
   But you won't be the death of me."

6. John Henry had a pretty little wife,
   The dress she wore was red.
   She said, "I'm going down to the C and O road,
   I'm going to find where John fell dead."

7. One day John Henry was missing,
   They all remembered his plan,
   They walked down the C and O line,
   They found him dead with the hammer in his hand.

8. . . . . About a mile from town,
   His head got cut off in the driving wheel
   And his body ain't never been found.

XXIV

This came from Albany, New York, from a woman who
knows "a lot more But i have a verry sick neice and all of
spair time with her if you Lik this all right i will send some
vearse." For some reason the lady never sent any more; so this
is all there is. I am sorry, for the first two of these three stanzas
are jewels. I have never seen them in any other version of
John Henry.

1. There was one mountain, and
   Mountain was so tall
   They sent for John Henry
   To come and blow the mountain small,
   Come blow the mountain small.

2. John Henry heard of a tunnel,
   I think it was under the ground.
   He said, "I'm goin' up there to cut a right-a-way
   So the train can make around,
   So the train can make around."

3. John Henry told his captain,
"A man ain't nothing but a man.
Before I'd be beat by your big steam drill
I'll die with this hammer in my hand,
I'll die with this hammer in my hand."

XXV

Gennett Record, 6005-A, carries the following song, known as *The Death of John Henry*. It is sung by Welby Toomey with fiddle and guitar accompaniment. Here John Henry dies an accidental death at the hand of his partner.

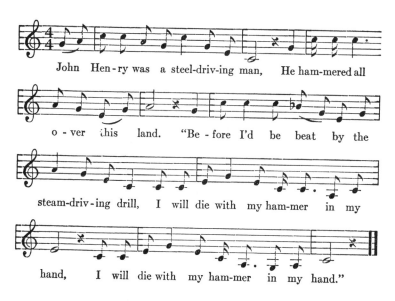

1. John Henry was a steel-driving man,
He hammered all over this land.
Before I'd be beat by the steam-driving drill
I will die with my hammer in my hand,
I will die with my hammer in my hand."

2. John Henry had a little woman,
   Her name was Mary Ann.
   When John Henry took sick and could not work
   She would go and drive steel like a man, *etc.*

3. John Henry had a partner
   That loved to drive steel all the while.
   But the first thing he did he let his hammer slip
   And he killed John Henry dead, *etc.*

4. They took John Henry to the white house
   And laid him in the sand.
   When people came around you would hear them say,
   "He sure was a steel-drivin' man," *etc.*

5. The women in Chicago heard of John Henry's death,
   All of them dressed up in red.
   When people asked them where they was a-goin':
   "We're goin' where John Henry fell dead," *etc.*

6. John Henry had a little woman,
   The dress she wore was blue.
   She went down the track and she never looked back,
   Sayin', "Johnny, I've been true to you," *etc.*

XXVI

This unusual version comes from Miss La Grange Haynes, Summerville, Georgia. She has known it twelve years. "An old Bachelor came through from Arkansas and spent the night with us. He gave us a Ballad of John Henry and a sketch story of his life." Here John Henry gets angry at his captain and shoots him. The ballad is mixed with other songs and several stanzas are much corrupted.

1. When John Henry was a boy
   Just about nine years old,
   He took his father's hammer and drove a hole in the wall,
   He said, "I'm gonna drive right here till I fall."

2. John Henry had a little woman,
   Her name was Paule Ann.
   John Henry took sick and had to go home,
   She drove a steel like a man.

3. John Henry said to the captain,
   "A man ain't nothing but a man,
   Before I let a man beat me down
   I will die with my hammer in my hand."

4. John Henry went to the captain's house,
   The captain was sleeping sound.
   He says, "Wake up, captain, wake up now,
   You ought to be dead and in the ground."

5. John Henry said to his captain,
   "When you go to town,
   Bring me back a ten-pound hammer,
   Goin' to beat that steel driver down."

6. John Henry came home one morning
   Just about four o'clock.
   He knock on the door and the door was locked.
   "There is something strange to me."

7. John Henry said to his captain,
   "What make you treat me so mean?
   I am going back to St. Augustine
   And work under a captain that don't treat me mean."

8. John Henry went to the captain's house,
   The captain was sleeping sound.
   He threw his gun on him and shot him in the side.
   Last word I heard the poor man say,
   "John Henry, you took my life."

9. They carried John Henry to the Colorado Mt.
   Where the rocks so hard and tall.
   The chilly wind did blow, the hammer did ring,
   John Henry laid down and cried.

10. When John Henry was on his death bed,
    His wife standing by his side,
    The last word I heard him say to her,
    "Give me a cool drink of water before I die."

11. I've been to the East and West,
    I've been to the North and South,
    I've been to the river and been baptized,
    I'm ready for my hole in the ground.

12. When John Henry was dead
    They buried him in the sand.
    People came from the East and West
    To see the steel-driving man.

13. John Henry said to his woman,
    "Where'd you get them new shoes?"
    "I got my shoes from a railroad man
    And my hat from a man in the mines."

14. When John Henry was on his death bed,
    People a-standing by his side,
    The last word I heard the poor boy say,
    "Take care of my wife and child."

15. John Henry had a little woman,
    Pretty as she could be.
    The last word I heard him say to her,
    "You're goin' to be the death of me."

XXVII

Down in a ditch fifteen feet deep, standing in muddy water
nearly knee-deep, hobble chains around their ankles, their
clothing soaked by a drizzling rain, half a dozen chain-gang
Negroes near Columbia, South Carolina, sang this one stanza
of *John Henry*. They evidently knew others, but the situation
was not exactly conducive to song. Then, too, their regular
song leader, a man named Britt, had made his escape two days

before; so they felt disorganized when it came to singing. When Dr. E. C. L. Adams, to whom I am indebted for aid during my quest around Columbia, asked the men where Britt was, one of them said, "Britt?—Cap'n, he takin' a little vacation."

John Hen-ry said to his Cap-tain, "A man ain't noth-in' but a man, And be-fore I'll let your steam drill beat me down, Die with the ham-mer in my hand, Die with the hammer in my hand."

1. John Henry said to his Captain,
   "A man ain't nothin' but a man,
   And before I'll let your steam drill beat me down,
   Die with the hammer in my hand,
   Die with the hammer in my hand."

XXVIII

From Big Bend Tunnel itself: I obtained this in June, 1927, at Talcott, West Virginia, from the singing of Thaddeus Campbell, a colored boy who helped me to get data on John Henry at Big Bend. He said that he had heard the old men sing this song ever since he could remember. He could not recall all of the stanzas, however. The tune is slow and hymn-like and is rather different from any of the other *John Henry* tunes I have heard.

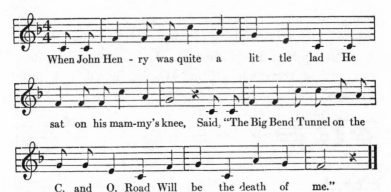

When John Hen - ry was quite a lit - tle lad He sat on his mam-my's knee, Said, "The Big Bend Tunnel on the C. and O. Road Will be the death of me."

1. When John Henry was quite a little lad
   He sat on his mammy's knee.
   Said, "The Big Bend Tunnel on the C. & O. Road
   Will be the death of me."

XXIX

This single stanza was sung by David Rushing, a student at Benedict College, Columbia, South Carolina, in February, 1927.

Old John Hen - ry said be - fore he died, "Well a man ain't noth-in' but a man, And be-fore I'd let a man beat me down, I'd die with the ham-mer in my hand, I'd die with the ham-mer in my hand."

1. Old John Henry said before he died,
   "Well a man ain't nothin' but a man,
   And before I'd let a man beat me down
   I'd die with the hammer in my hand,
   I'd die with the hammer in my hand."

XXX

For comparative purposes, I quote a phonograph version of
John Hardy from Columbia Record, 167-D, sung by Eva Davis
with banjo accompaniment. The tune is almost identical with
the tune of *John Hardy* given by Campbell and Sharp in their
English Folk Songs from the Southern Appalachians, p. 257.
These two are the only tunes of *John Hardy* available at present. The phonograph record is an excellent reproduction of
the mountain singer's way of rendering *John Hardy*.

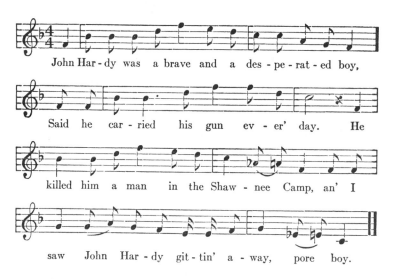

John Har-dy was a brave and a des-pe-rat-ed boy,
Said he car-ried his gun ev-er' day. He
killed him a man in the Shaw-nee Camp, an' I
saw John Har-dy git-tin' a-way, pore boy.

1. John Hardy was a brave and a desperated boy,
   Said he carried his gun ever' day.
   He killed him a man in the Shawnee Camp,
   An' I saw John Hardy gittin' away, pore boy.

2. They arrested him down at the Big Ben' Tunnel
   An' they carried him back to Welch,
   Says, "There is no bail for the murder of a man,"
   An' they locked John Hardy back in jail, pore boy.

3. John Hardy's friends, they were standing around,
   Said, "I'm 'fraid John Hardy's going to hang."
   Well, the judge turned around and he looked on his book,
   "John Hardy is sentenced to be hung, pore boy."

4. John Hardy's father, he was standing by,
   "O John, what have you done?"
   "I killed my partner for fifteen cents
   An' today I'm condemned to be hung, pore boy."

5. John Hardy's mother was standing by,
   "O John, what have you done?"
   "All for the sake of that black-eyed girl
   That John Hardy never lied to his gun, pore boy."

6. I've been to the East and I've been to the West,
   I've travelled this wide world around.
   I've been to the river and I've been baptized
   An' today I'm on my hangun' ground, Lord, Lord.

7. "O sister, O sister, come stand by my side
   For the day is drawing on.
   You never shall forget these words you heard
   When you hear John Hardy's song, Lord, Lord.

8. "When this black cap is put over my face
   No more shall I see;
   An' when I am in my silent tomb,
   Will you sometimes think of me, Lord, Lord?"

9. John Hardy had one pretty little miss,
   She always dressed in lace.
   Well, she walked right down on the hangun' ground,
   "O Johnny, I wish I could kiss your face, pore boy."

I have a few more variants of *John Henry,* but there is nothing to be gained by quoting all. These variants, some of them fragmentary, are from the following places: Chapel Hill, North Carolina (2); Durham, North Carolina; Morganton, North Carolina; Edisto Island, South Carolina; Fenwick Island, South Carolina; Covington, Georgia (3); Birmingham, Alabama: Salt Lake City, Utah; Jacksonville, Florida; Chicago, Illinois (2).

Among these the only stanzas not ordinarily found are the following:

> John Henry had a little wife
> And she lived by the riverside.
> When she heard John Henry was dead,
> Lord, she hung her head and cried,
> Lord, she hung her head and cried.
> —Jacksonville, Florida.

> Hear that hammer that keeps on ringing,
> Hear that hammer that keeps on ringing,
> That's John Henry singing,
> "I'll die with the hammer in my hand,
> I'll die with the hammer in my hand."
> —Chicago, Illinois.

> John Henry hammered in the mountains
> Way in the north end of town.
> The womans all laid their heads in the windows
> When he laid his hammer down.
> —Chicago, Illinois.

Now that the reader has had an opportunity to examine this array of *John Henry* ballads, a brief discussion of their interrelations is in order. A survey of all the *John Henry* ballads now available, fifty in all,[8] shows that certain stanzas

[8] Counting those published in this volume and elsewhere, plus several unpublished variants in my possession, but excluding fragmentary variants.

tend to occur over and over. However, there are three which occur more frequently than any others. The following stanza or a close variant of it occurs thirty-two times in the fifty ballads:

> John Henry said to his captain,
> "A man ain't nothing but a man,
> And before I'd let your steam drill beat me down,
> I'd die with the hammer in my hand."

The stanza,

> John Henry was a little boy,
> Sitting on his papa's knee, *etc.*

or a near variant of it, runs a close second, occurring thirty times out of a possible fifty. The third place is held by that stanza which sets forth that John Henry's woman wore a red dress and that she was going where her man fell dead. It occurs twenty-four times.[9] These three stanzas appear in combination frequently. Designating them as A, B, and C, respectively, we may represent these frequencies as follows:

A and B occur in same ballad 18 times out of a possible 30.

A and C occur in same ballad 17 times out of a possible 24.

B and C occur in same ballad 14 times out of a possible 24.

In other words, these particular stanzas occur in combination oftener than they would by mere chance, this fact suggesting that they originated together and have tended to travel together ever since.

More can be said now about the diffusion of Blankenship's ballad. His stanza 1 has no parallel in any of the forty-nine other variants of *John Henry* now available. Stanza 2 is almost identical with the A to which I referred above as being the most frequent stanza of all. It is important, however, to note that Blankenship's stanza reads (italics mine):

[9] The "blue dress" stanza is not so popular, for it occurs only twelve times.

John Henry said to his captain:
"You are nothing but a common man,
Before that steam drill shall beat me down,
I'll die with with my hammer in my hand."

Now, the second line of this stanza never occurs in any of the other ballads. In the others it is always,

"A man ain't nothing but a man."

A small matter, apparently, but it is really significant that the "you-are-nothing-but-a-common-man" form occurs once, while the other form occurs thirty-one times. It appears to me indisputable that Blankenship's stanza came later than, and was modeled on, the other; and that it could never overcome the start which the other had. "A man ain't nothing but a man" just naturally sounds better to the ballad singer.

Stanza 3 of Blankenship has no approximate parallel in any of the other ballads. Variants of stanza 4 occur five times. Stanzas 5 and 6 are not found in any of the other versions. Stanza 7 is approximated very closely nine times. Stanza 8 does not occur outside of Blankenship. A close variant of stanza 9 occurs once, in a ballad from Summerville, Georgia. Stanza 10 never occurs in whole as Blankenship wrote it, but the first two lines of it are found fifteen times in other variants of *John Henry*:

John Henry had a little woman,
Her name was Pollie Ann.

Stanza 11 as a unit is paralleled only once, but the fourth line,

"I am going where John Henry fell dead,"

occurs some twenty-five times in other variants. Similarly, in stanza 12, line 1 will be found twice in the other variants of

John Henry, but the lines about the wife dressed in blue say-ing, "John Henry, I've been true to you," are very common outside of Blankenship. Here again it is probably a case of Blankenship's having based his stanza on one already in circulation.

These facts support the theory that Blankenship's ballad came on the scene long after most of the *John Henry* stanzas had become "set," and that it has made very little impression upon the diffusion of *John Henry.* In this connection it is in-teresting to note further that the "sat-on-his-papa's-knee" stanza and the "dress-she-wore-was-red" stanza do not occur at all in Blankenship, and the frequency of their occurrence suggests that they were in circulation before Blankenship's ballad. If the hypothetical original printed *John Henry* ballad is ever found, I should expect to find in it these two stanzas together with the "man-ain't-nothing-but-a-man" stanza.

Any folk song undergoes changes of various kinds as it passes from one person to another through oral communica-tion. New variants arise, some of them straying so far from the original as to constitute virtually distinct songs. Sometimes highly corrupt or vulgar variants grow up and crowd out the respectable versions among certain types of singers. *John Henry,* perhaps because it is of rather recent origin, has so far undergone relatively little corruption. Of course, there are end-less variations of minor points to be found in the variants of this ballad, and there are several instances of new lines grow-ing out of a singer's misunderstanding of the correct lines, but for the most part *John Henry* has stood the wear exceedingly well. There are undoubtedly some vulgar versions[10] of *John*

[10] Realizing that *John Henry* contains excellent symbolism from the Freud-ian point of view, I have kept a watch for such versions, but I have never heard one. However, Prof. English Bagby, of the Department of Psychology of the University of North Carolina, tells me that he has talked to at least one Negro who definitely interpreted *John Henry* in terms of sexual symbolism.

Henry in circulation, but none has ever fallen into my net. I can truthfully say that the following stanzas contain the only "low-down" I have ever heard on John Henry.

> John Henry had a little woman,
> Name was Ida Red.
> John Henry had a little woman,
> She sleeps in my own bed.
> > —Covington, Georgia, 1925.

> Old John Henry was a railroad man,
> Washed his face in the frying pan,
> Combed his head with the wagon wheel,
> Died with the toothache in his heel.
> > —Covington, Georgia, 1925.

> Uncle John Henry's dead,
> And the last words he said was,
> "Never let your woman
> Have her way."

> John Henry told his captain,
> "If you have to go to town,
> Bring me back a ten-pound hammer—
> Dat man give Delia Ann a gown."

> I'm going up Decatur,
> Coming down Broad,
> Looking for the woman
> Don't wear no drawers a-tall.

> Going up Decatur
> With my hat in my hand,
> Looking for the woman
> What ain't got no man.

> Makes no difference
> What your mamma said,
> Going to have my easy ride
> Until I'm dead.
> > —Covington, Georgia, 1925.

CHAPTER VIII

JOHN HENRY, THE HERO

ALL QUESTIONS of authenticity of the John Henry tradition fade into insignificance before the incontrovertible fact that for his countless admirers John Henry is a reality. To them he will always be a hero, an idol, a symbol of the "natural" man.

It is often charged against the Negro that he glorifies his tough characters, his "bad men." But when one considers that the Negro has had little opportunity to develop outside the fields of labor and hell-raising, this tendency is not surprising. Bad men are nearly always interesting, and, incidentally, no one can sing of them any more heartily than the white man. But a working man fits into the drab scene of everyday life, and it is a miracle if he achieves any sort of notoriety by his hard labor. John Henry, then, is a hero indeed. With his hammer and his determination to prove his superiority over a machine, he made a name for himself in folk history. His superstrength, his grit, his endurance, and his martyrdom appeal to something fundamental in the heart of the common man. John Henry stands for something which the pick-and-shovel Negro idolizes—brute strength. He epitomizes the tragedy of man versus machine. In laying down his life for the sake of convincing himself and others that he could beat a machine, he did something which many a Negro would gladly do. The whole thing is a sort of alluring tragedy which appeals strongly to one's egotism.

So strong, indeed, has been the admiration, the envy, of other men for John Henry that some have tried to repeat his drama. I have no doubt but that some of these John Henry episodes said to have happened at so many places throughout the country (the Alabama episode, for instance) are based on real incidents in which would-be John Henry's did their best to put themselves beside the god of the hammer.

Mention John Henry to a group of Negro working men and the chances are that you start an admiration contest. The rare man who intimates that *he* could beat John Henry is laughed down by his fellows. "Why, man," said a true John Henryite on such an occasion, "John Henry could take that hammer between his teeth and drive with his hands tied and beat you like all git-out." "Yes, Lawd," affirmed another, "that man had a stroke like a Alabama mule." "They tells me," said a third, "that he used to keep six men runnin' just to carry his drills back and forth from the man that sharpened 'em." And so on until no one could think of anything else to say about him.

F. P. Barker, an old Alabama steel driver who claimed to have known John Henry, said, "I could drive from both shoulders myself, and I was as far behind John Henry as the moon is behind the sun. The world has not yet produced a man to whip steel like John Henry."

A young woman in Georgia concluded an account of John Henry's life as follows:

When he died people came from all parts of the world to see this Famous man John Henry. his wife had it engraved on his tombstone

his Epitah
"Here lies the steel driving man."

John Henry has a way of cropping up at unexpected times and places. I was standing on the street at Chapel Hill one night in a throng of people gathered to hear the Dempsey-Sharkey fight on the radio. When things looked bad for Dempsey, a Negro man who stood near me began to show his displeasure. "If they'd put old Jack Johnson in there," he said, "he'd lay that Sharkey man out." At the end of the round we discussed colored prize fighters. Suddenly he came out with, "I'll tell you another colored man would've made a real prize fighter—that's John Henry. Yessir, anybody that could handle a thirty-pound hammer like that man could would make a sure-'nough fighter."

There is, on the whole, a surprisingly small amount of exaggeration in the stories about John Henry told by those who worship at his shrine. Occasionally you hear that John Henry used a thirty-pound hammer or that he wore out six shakers on the day of the famous contest or that his statue has been carved in solid rock at the portal of Big Bend Tunnel, but around John Henry there has not yet grown up a body of fantastic lore like that which surrounds certain other folk characters—Paul Bunyan, for example. The only really bizarre tale I have ever heard about John Henry is one which Professor Howard W. Odum obtained from a construction-camp Negro at Chapel Hill three years ago. I repeat it here just as it was published in *Negro Workaday Songs*.

One day John Henry lef' rock quarry on way to camp an' had to go through woods an' fiel'. Well, he met big black bear an' didn't do nothin' but shoot 'im wid his bow an' arrer, an' arrer went clean through bear an' stuck in big tree on other side. So John Henry pulls arrer out of tree an' pull so hard he falls back 'gainst 'nother tree which is so full o' flitterjacks, an' first tree is full o' honey, an' in pullin' arrer out o' one he shaken down honey, an' in fallin' 'gainst other he shaken down flitterjacks. Well, John Henry set there an' et honey an' flitterjacks an' set there an' et honey an' flitterjacks, an' after while when he went to get up to go, button pop off'n his pants an' kill a rabbit mo' 'n a hundred ya'ds on other side o' de tree. An' so up jumped brown baked pig wid sack o' biscuits on his back, an' John Henry et him too.

So John Henry gits up to go on through woods to camp for supper, 'cause he 'bout to be late an' he mighty hongry for his supper. John Henry sees lake down hill and thinks he'll get him a drink o' water, cause he's thirsty, too, after eatin' honey an' flitterjacks an' brown roast pig an' biscuits, still he's hongry yet. An' so he goes down to git drink water an' finds lake ain't nothin' but lake o' honey, an' out in middle dat lake ain't nothin' but tree full o' biscuits. An' so John Henry don't do nothin' but drink dat lake o' honey dry. An' he et the tree full o' biscuits, too. An' so 'bout that time it begin' to git dark, an' John Henry sees light on hill an' he think maybe he can git sumpin to eat, cause he's mighty hongry after big day drillin'. So he look 'roun' an' see light on hill an' runs up to house where light is an' ast people livin' dere, why'n hell dey don't give him sumpin' to eat, 'cause he ain't had much. An' so he et dat, too.

Gee-hee, hee, dat nigger could eat! But dat ain't all, cap'n. Dat nigger could wuk mo' 'n he could eat. He's greates' steel driller ever live, regular giaunt, he was; could drill wid his hammer mo' 'n two steam drills, an' some say mo' 'n ten. Always beggin' boss to git 'im bigger hammer. John Henry wus cut out fer big giaunt driller. One day when he wus jes' few weeks ol' settin' on his mammy's knee he commence cryin' an' his mommer say, "John Henry, whut's matter, little son?" An' he up an' say right den an' dere dat nine-poun' hammer be death o' him. An' sho' 'nough he grow up right 'way into bigges' steel driller worl' ever see. Why dis I's tellin' you now wus jes' when he's young fellow; waits til' I tells you 'bout his drillin' in mountains an' in Pennsylvania. An' so one day he drill all way from Rome, Georgia, to D'catur, mo' 'n a hundred miles drillin' in one day, an' I ain't sure dat was his bes' day. No, I ain't sure dat wus his bes' day.

But, boss, John Henry was a regular boy, not lak some o' dese giaunts you read 'bout not likin' wimmin an' nothin'. John Henry love to come to town same as any other nigger, only mo' so. Co'se he's mo' important an' all dat, an' co'se he had mo' wimmin 'an anybody else, some say mo' 'n ten, but as to dat I don't know. I means, boss, mo' wimmen 'an ten men, 'cause, Lawd, I specs he had mo' 'n thousand wimmin'. An' John Henry was a great co'tin man, too, cap'n. Always wus dat way. Why, one day when he settin' by his pa' in san' out in front o' de house, jes' few weeks old, women come along and claim him fer deir man. An' dat's funny, too, but it sho' was dat way all his life. An' so when he come to die John Henry had mo' wimmin, all dressed in red an' blue an' all dem fine colors come to see him dead, if it las' thing dey do, an' wus mighty sad sight, people all standin' 'roun', both cullud an' white.

The diffusion of the John Henry tradition among the Negro folk of all sections of the nation and, incidentally, among a large proportion of the white population, is a phenomenon of no mean importance. Even with my limited means of collecting data on John Henry I have come into the possession of something about him from practically every section of the United States. On the sea-islands of South Carolina, supposedly among the most isolated sections of this country, I found John Henry quite commonly known. On St. Helena Island it was no trouble at all to pick up three or four persons who could sing *John Henry*. On Edisto Island I stopped the first man I saw carrying a guitar and asked him to play *John Henry*. All he needed was a knife, and as soon as he had borrowed one from the gentleman who accompanied me, he sat down on the roadside and made his "box" talk *John Henry* in an enchanting fashion.

On Fenwick Island, one of the most isolated of all the sea-islands, lying between Edisto and St. Helena, occurred an incident which I shall never forget. I relate it here because it shows so clearly the hold which John Henry takes on the mind of the naïve Negro folk. I had gone to Fenwick to make some comparative observations during my work on the Social Science Research Council's *Study of Negro Culture on St. Helena Island*. Taking a long chance on the weather, my guide, Manny Campbell, and I made the trip of three miles from Edisto to Fenwick in a rowboat. Landing on Fenwick we made our way to a small group of cabins—all that remained of a once prosperous sea-island cotton community. The air was still and heavy, an ideal day for that nuisance of the islands, the sand fly. Here and there groups of people were hovering over smoking fires, trying to escape the pest. We approached a group of women and children—most of the men and a great many of the women were in the fields—and made ourselves acquainted. After convincing them, I think somewhat to their disappointment, that I had no medicines to sell, I turned the conversation to animal stories. But it was not exactly a propitious time for a collector of folklore. Sand flies and folklore don't mix so well.

Suddenly a stiff, cold wind came from the north, and a few moments later the rain began to fall in torrents. With shouts of glee the Negroes ran inside, thankful that nature had ousted the sand flies. Manny and I took refuge in a two-room cabin where two women and several children were sitting around an open fire, trying to keep warm this time. With the help of Manny, I soon got one of the women to "talk some ol' storee." I was delighted with the turn of events.

This good fortune did not last long. George White, husband of the story-teller, came in from the field wet and disgusted, dampening the spirit of the party. There was too much rain, the rain was going to rot the potatoes, the cabbage and lettuce were going to ruin, the whole damned island was a hell of a place. He dragged a box from the other room and sat on it in the chimney corner. After his temper had cooled a little, his wife reminded him that it would be a good idea for him to row down to Bennett's Point for some supplies.

"We got grits, enty?" said White. "We can git along till tomorrow."

His wife was silent for a few minutes, then she again suggested the need of food for the family.

"Great Gawd!" growled George, "go out in dis wedder? Not me, I got enough o' boats for a w'ile." He launched into a story of a row-boat trip which he had made a short time previous to this. He had rowed all day and half of the night, he said, moving his family, his household goods, and several pigs and chickens in an eighteen-foot boat to Fenwick Island.

"My hands ain't got over it yet," he said, displaying his hands. He continued dramatically, "W'en I got here my hands was gripped to dem oar jus' like dat. Man, I couldn't even turn dem oar a-loose. Dey had to take 'em out o' my hands for me."

"T'ink of ol' John Henry," said his wife. "If he could die wid dat hammer in his hand, you ought not to fuss about rowin' two mile to git us somethin' to eat."

"Dat's all right," replied George, "but I ain't a-gwine a-die wid no *oar* in my hand if I can help it!"

At mention of John Henry my spirits went up considerably. I had only been waiting for an auspicious moment to bring him in myself. When the laughter over George's drollery had subsided, I professed an interested ignorance about John Henry. George White was like a different person. He wanted to talk John Henry. Getting up from his box-seat, he began to tell how he heard of John Henry from a man who had worked on the Charleston-Savannah highway. As his story progressed, George grow more and more eloquent. He stood behind the dining table, wet slouch hat hanging down over one eye, acting out his story as he went. To him John Henry was a spike driver, of course. What would a sea-islander know of rock drilling?

"It was de flesh ag'in' de steam," he concluded. "De flesh ag'in' de steam. An' jus' as John Henry drove dat las' spike he drop dead right where he stan' wid de hammer in his han'."

Manny seemed thrilled but saddened by this tale. It was his introduction to John Henry, and White's telling of the story had made a deep impression on him. He had encouraged the narrator with frequent interjections such as "dat's right" and "Lawd-Jeesus!" At the climax he had stared, wide-eyed, for several seconds.

John Henry was a magic wand. George White was more than pleased with himself. He consented to "talk ol' storee," and later I saw him in his boat pulling for Bennett's Point.

Crossing back to Edisto Island was not exactly a pleasure. Wind and tide were against us, and a cold rain soaked us. In the middle of the Edisto the waves began to break over the side of the boat, and for every foot gained we seemed to go back two. Manny cast apprehensive glances over his shoulder to the "big house" where we wanted to land, now barely visible in the gathering darkness.

"Going to make it?" I asked.

"Yes-suh! I jus' been study about dat John Henry. If dat man could beat de steam, I t'ink I bring dis ol' boat back to dat landin' all right. If I don't, I'll die wid dese oar in my hand." With a determination like that of John Henry, he bucked the wind and waves, and thirty minutes later we were in calmer water.

"Lawd-Jeesus," exclaimed Manny when we were almost to land, "I can't stop t'ink about dat John Henry man. Drivin' ag'in' de steam. Which one drive hund'ed spikes first? I specs John Henry beat de steam by about *one* spike, enty?"

Thus does the story of John Henry, half a century after its origin, continue to capture the imagination of those who hear it for the first time. There is enough tragedy, enough humor, enough heroism in it to make it a story which will last.

His lineage unknown, his reality disputed, his grave unmarked, John Henry's spirit goes marching on. His name is sung from a thousand dusky lips every day. That is not such a bad monument for a Negro steel driver.

I marvel that some of the "new" Negroes with an artistic bent do not exploit the wealth of John Henry lore. Here is material for an epic poem, for a play, for an opera, for a Negro symphony. What more tragic theme than the theme of John Henry's martydom? Picture the awfulness of the scene when

> He broke a rib in his left-han' side,
> And his intrels fell on the groun',

or the wishful grandeur of

> They took John Henry to the White House
> And buried him in the san',
> And every locomotive come roarin' by
> Says, "There lays that steel-drivin' man,
> There lays that steel-drivin' man."

Perhaps the sculptor is most to be envied, for he can bring to a realization that phantasy of a Negro pick-and-shovel man who said, "Cap'n, I seen John Henry's statue cut out'n solid rock at the mouth o' Big Ben' Tunnel. Yes, sir, there he stan' with the hammer in his han'—in solid rock."

Maybe there was no John Henry. One can easily doubt it. But there is a vivid, fascinating, tragic legend about him which Negro folk have kept alive and have cherished for more than half a century, and in so doing they have enriched the cultural life of America.

BIBLIOGRAPHY OF JOHN HENRY[1]

BOOKS

Burlin, Natalie Curtis, *Negro Folk-Songs,* Hampton Series. G. Schirmer, New York City, 1918-19. In vol. IV is an excellent hammer song version of *John Henry* with music.

Campbell, Olive Dame, and Sharp, Cecil J., *English Folk Songs from the Southern Appalachians.* G. P. Putnam's Sons, New York City, 1917. No 87 is a variant of *John Hardy* with music.

Cox, John H., *Folk-Songs of the South.* Harvard University Press, 1925. On pp. 175-88 is found Cox's discussion of *John Hardy.* Nine variants of *John Hardy,* one of which is really a *John Henry.*

Handy, W. C., *Blues.* Albert & Charles Boni, New York, 1926. Part of *John Henry Blues,* pp. 135-38, is based on a folk version of the hammer song. This was previously published in sheet music form in 1922 by the W. C. Handy Co., of New York City. On the inside front cover of the sheet music, Handy printed a statement signed by Phil H. Brown, a Washington, D. C., Negro, formerly of Kentucky, purporting to give the true story of John Henry.

[1] Includes references to John Hardy also. Several feature stories about John Henry, written by the author and published in a large number of newspapers, white and Negro, are omitted. They were written largely to stimulate interest in John Henry and to aid in securing data, and they contributed nothing new to the subject. A few references which merely mention *John Henry* or *John Hardy* songs as being present in certain places are omitted from the regular bibliography. These are: *Berea Quarterly,* October, 1915, p. 20 ("John Henry, *or* The Steam Drill," mentioned from Kentucky); F. C. Brown, "Ballad Literature in North Carolina," in *Proceedings and Addresses of the Fifteenth Annual Session of the Literary and Historical Association of North Carolina,* 1914, p. 12 (*John Hardy* named as sung in North Carolina); J. H. Cox, *Journal of American Folk-Lore,* XXIX, 400 (*John Hardy* mentioned from West Virginia); J. H. Cox, *West Virginia School Journal and Educator,* XLV, 160 (*John Hardy* mentioned in West Virginia); H. C. Davis, *Journal of American Folk-Lore,* XXVII, 249 (*John Henry* hammer song mentioned from South Carolina); H. G. Shearin and J. H. Combs, *A Syllabus of Kentucky Folk-Songs,* p. 19 (both *John Henry* and *John Hardy* cited as present in Kentucky).

Johnson, Guy B., "John Henry: A Negro Legend." In *Ebony and Topaz,* edited by Charles S. Johnson, Opportunity Publishing Co., National Urban League, New York City, 1927. A general discussion of the legend. One variant of the ballad, one of the hammer songs, with tunes. Both are included in present work.

Odum, Howard W., and Johnson, Guy B., *Negro Workaday Songs.* University of North Carolina Press, Chapel Hill, 1926. Chapter XIII is entitled, "John Henry: Epic of the Negro Workingman." Eleven Southern variants of the ballad, four hammer songs, with general discussion. A tune on page 248.

Sandburg, Carl, *The American Songbag.* Harcourt, Brace and Co., New York, 1927. A twelve-stanza variant of *John Henry* appears on pp. 24-5. The tune is the same as that in Sandburg's article in *Country Gentleman,* April, 1927. The harmonization, however, is poor from the standpoint of Negro flavor. Other *John Henry* references in this valuable book are: *Drivin' Steel,* p. 150; *If I Die a Railroad Man,* p. 362; *Ever Since Uncle John Henry Been Dead,* p. 376; *My Old Hammah,* p. 457.

Scarborough, Dorothy, *On the Trail of Negro Folk-Songs.* Harvard University Press, 1925, pp. 218-22. Six hammer songs, one tune, brief comments on John Henry, whom Miss Scarborough, following Cox, appears to identify with John Hardy.

Talley, Thomas W., *Negro Folk Rhymes.* Macmillan, New York City, 1922. One variant of *John Henry,* p. 105.

White, Newman I., *American Negro Folk-Songs.* Harvard University Press, 1928. The best general work on Negro songs yet published. Three *John Henry* ballad variants, several hammer-song types, one tune. This book came too late to be quoted in the present volume. It is interesting that White (pp. 189-90) and the present writer reached, independently, identical conclusions as to the relation of John Henry and John Hardy.

PERIODICALS

Bascom, Louise Rand, "Ballads and Songs of Western North Carolina," *Journal of American Folk-Lore,* XXII, 247-49. One variant of *John Hardy,* also mention of *John Henry* as being sung in the mountains of western North Carolina.

Berea Quarterly, October, 1910, p. 26. A fragment of *John Hardy* from Kentucky.

Cox, John H., "John Hardy," *Journal of American Folk-Lore,* XXXII, 505-20. Here Cox first discussed the origin of *John Hardy,* regarding *John Henry* as a variant of it. Five variants of *Hardy.* In his later work, *Folk-Songs of the South,* practically all of the discussion is reprinted and four more variants are published. Variant E had previously been published in the *West Virginia School Journal and Educator,* XLIV, 216, and *Journal of American Folk-Lore,* XXVI, 180.

Cox, John H., "The Yew Pine Mountain," *American Speech,* February, 1927, pp. 226-27. The *Henry-Hardy* problem is mentioned incidentally, Cox indicating that he has revised his earlier opinion. One new variant of *John Hardy.*

Johnson, Guy B., "John Henry," *Southern Workman,* April, 1927, pp. 158-60. A brief appreciative discussion of the John Henry legend.

Lomax, J. A., "Some Types of American Folk-Song," *Journal of American Folk-Lore,* XVIII, 14. An excellent variant of *John Henry,* reported to have been heard in Kentucky and West Virginia.

Perrow, E. C., "Songs and Rhymes from the South," *Journal of American Folk-Lore,* XXVI, 123-73. Four hammer songs, one with tune, and one ballad, pp. 163-65, from Mississippi, Tennessee, Kentucky, and Indiana.

Sandburg, Carl, "Songs of the Old Frontiers," *Country Gentleman,* April, 1927. This article contains one *John Henry* ballad, with music.

PHONOGRAPH RECORDS[2]

Brunswick, 112-A, *Death of John Henry (Steel Driving Man)*. Uncle Dave Macon, voice and banjo. Guitar by Sam McGee.

Brunswick, 177-A, *The Nine Pound Hammer*. Al Hopkins and His Buckle Busters. A work song type in a quartet arrangement.

Columbia, 15019-D, *John Henry*. Gid Tanner and Riley Puckett.

Columbia, 15142-D, *John Henry (The Steel Drivin' Man)*. Gid Tanner and His Skillet-Lickers. Tune same as in 15019-D. Two new stanzas added. More orchestral work in this record than in 15019-D.

Columbia, 167-D, *John Hardy*. Eva Davis, solo with banjo accompaniment.

Gennett, 6005-A, *The Death of John Henry*. Welby Toomey, fiddle and guitar accompaniment.

Okeh, 45101, *John Henry Blues*. Earl Johnson and His Dixie Entertainers, singing with fiddle, guitar, and banjo accompaniment.

Silvertone, 5002, *Death of John Henry*. Welby Toomey. Same as Gennett, 6005-A.

Silvertone, 3662, *John Henry*. Gibbs and Watson. Same as Columbia, 15019-D.

Victor, 19824, *Water Boy*. Paul Robeson. One stanza is very similar in words and tune to the hammer song (A in Chap. VI) from Big Bend Tunnel.

Vocalion, A-1094, *John Henry*. Henry Thomas ("Ragtime Texas"), voice, whistling, and guitar.

[2] There are probably a few more *John Henry* records among some of the lesser brands, but these are all that a reasonably thorough search has brought to my attention.